GW00775842

CAN━━━━━━

BOOK SALE

# SHADES OF LOVE

*She whirled to face him. He stopped
dead in his tracks, his easy smile fading....*

Elizabeth Everett is an advertising genius –
there is no one better at delivering the
copywriting goods that keep her one step
ahead of her colleagues.

Her love life, however, is a very different
matter. Tall, plain and ungainly, how can
Elizabeth ever hope to capture the heart
of Tom Carey? Particularly when her
arch-rival Melanie – the beautiful rising
star of Elizabeth's most lucrative advertising campaign – is making it clear that she
has a prior claim.

But when Elizabeth meets the enigmatic,
and blind, John DiMarco she is forced to
re-evaluate herself. And how other see her.

# SHADES OF LOVE

# SHADES OF LOVE

## Vera Cowie

**Severn House Large Print**
London & New York

This first world edition published in Great Britain 2001 by
SEVERN HOUSE LARGE PRINT BOOKS LTD of
9-15, High Street, Sutton, Surrey, SM1 1DF.
This first world edition published in the USA 2001 by
SEVERN HOUSE PUBLISERS INC., of
595 Madison Avenue, New York, NY 10022

British Library Cataloguing in Publication Data

Cowie, Vera, 1928 -
    Shades of love. - Large print ed.
    1. Love stories  2. Large type books
    I. Title
    823.9 ' 14 [F]

    ISBN  0-7278-7027-0

All situations in this pub
any resemblance to livin

Printed and bound in G
MPG Books Ltd, Bodm

# One

"Liz! At long last! Welcome back from the outback!"

Elizabeth Everett smiled wanly. She was glad to be back, but this was her third such greeting since pushing through the swing doors of the modern glass box on the Vauxhall Bridge Road which housed the offices of Brittan, Barnes & Beckwith, the advertising agency for which she had worked for the past seven years as, John Brittan was wont to say with pride, 'their hot shot copy-writer'.

Now she hugged and kissed Bertie Fry, her oldest friend and original mentor at the agency; a huggable bear of a man who had taken the fledgling under his wing only to see her outgrow and outfly him.

"It's great to be back, Bertie. How are things with the team?

He laid a finger to his nose. "There have been developments while you have been

7

sunning yourself on Bondi Beach."

"Sunning myself!" Liz thought of the six months hard grind she had just completed, helping to start the new Australian branch off on the right foot. "Chance would be a fine thing. And what developments?"

"The Yanks are coming – or rather they have arrived, in the shape of our brand new Creative Director. One Thomas Carey."

"What happened to Bill Sampson?"

"Couldn't handle Melanie."

"Who can, these days?"

"Our new boss. Rumour has it he was brought all the way across the Atlantic to do just that."

Liz looked doubtful. In her time she had seen a whole procession of not only Account and Group but also Creative Directors come and go. "What sort of a miracle worker has Uncle Fred Barnes hired this time?"

"Somebody head-hunted from the mighty Hendricks-Mahon in New York."

Liz raised her eyebrows. "Why would anyone in their right minds want to leave them?"

"Because, according to the grapevine, Uncle Fred has offered a free hand at BB&B, which could, of course, have something to do with the fact that more than one of H.M's big-bucks clients followed our American friend across the Atlantic. Figures like one hundred million dollars are being bandied about. That says something loud and clear, I think. Whatever, he is now overlord of every prime account we have – including that prime of primes, *L'amoreuse*, which is about to unveil its new make-up range to accompany the perfume for which you wrote that memorable and oh-so-successful shout-line. I think he has been hanging on for your return because, so far, everything is still on the starting blocks. If he doesn't bring you in on it then he's not the whiz-kid we have all been led to believe."

Liz appreciated the flattery, but in seven years she had seen many a Catherine-wheel start end in a damp squib finish.

"I mean," Bertie went on, "how many copy-writers get to accompany the boss in establishing a new branch? That fact alone makes it clear how highly John Brittan thinks of you. Besides, word of your prowess has by now reached the new boy from every floor in this building – apart from all those clever words you wrote in your copy, of course." Bertie punched her lightly on the shoulder. "He's not the only one glad you're back. The place hasn't been the same without you. Luigi's at lunchtime as usual? I want to hear all about the new Australian branch …"

"Which, when I left, was about to bear fruit," quipped Liz over her shoulder as she left the lift at her floor.

Entering her office, she exhaled a pleasurable sigh. It was good to be back, to see that everything was as she had left it; large, neat and tidy. Just like her. She had placed her desk at one end by the wall, her drawing board at the other end by the big windows, where it got all the light. Someone had put a large bunch of flowers in one of her large stone pencil jars, and above it hung a banner proclaiming *WELCOME HOME 'OUR MISS EVERETT'*, the words in quotes being what John Brittan was wont to call her possessively, whenever he was extolling her virtues to prospective clients.

Liz smiled, bending to smell the flowers, touched by the gesture. She was happy to be back home again and, though she sighed at the pile of letters, files and reports sitting on her desk top, she was pleased that in spite of six months away her input still mattered. Pulling out her chair she immersed herself in sorting through the pile, and almost the first thing she came across, among the proof copies of various new ads, was one for Mila Frey shoes. Obviously one of our American friend's old faithfuls, she thought, since the account was unknown to her. It was a full-colour glossy of several pairs of exquisite female legs, photographed from the knee downwards, their stance making it plain the women were having a confidential gossip. Each pair of elegant feet wore the very latest, to-die-for Mila Frey handmade shoes, exquisitely shaped, stiletto-heeled, the ultimate in high-fashion, and the shout-line was *Let your shoes do the talking.*

Nice, thought Liz, impressed. Very nice indeed. So was the list of magazines scheduled to carry the campaign. Every single one of the expensive glossies; but then, if you could afford the shoes the magazines were loose change.

She was catching up on the latest quarterly report on billings and placings when her door opened and a voice trilled: "So how did you find all those gorgeous, bronzed Aussies, then?"

The woman who was the face and body behind the ultra-exclusive and astronomically priced perfume named *L'amoreuse*, BB&B's biggest and most important account, undulated into the room. She perched on the edge of Liz's desk, hitching her already miniscule skirt to do so, revealing another six inches of legs that were worth every inch of exposure.

"Hello, Melanie," Liz said non-committally, riding the swell of bitchery.

"I don't see any signs of a tan. Don't tell me you didn't take advantage of every spare minute you had to don your bikini and go and sun yourself at Bondi?"

Since Liz never wore a bathing suit if she could help it, which Melanie knew only too well, she knew she was in for a double-dose of Melanie's spite. After all, she had been away for six months.

Melanie and Liz had known and disliked each other for some years, ever since Liz, newly down from Cambridge with a First in English, had been accepted as the fourth in the Redcliffe Gardens flat where Melanie, then an aspiring actress, was already in residence. She had taken one look at the Amazonian Liz; five feet ten inches tall, big-boned, eleven stone and a standard size sixteen, and honed in at once, instantly aware of the way the other girl's economy-size packaging pointed up her own band-box fragility.

Melanie was five feet four, seven and a half stone and a size ten, with curves resembling a scenic railway. She was also ravishingly pretty, with a face the camera worshipped: a perfect heart-shape, with a skin like a newly opened camellia under a cloud of blue-black hair that shone like polished silk. Her eyes were a matched set of star sapphires, with silk fringes for lashes, and she had a mouth that sent the average man's fantasies into overdrive. That there was little behind the splendour made no difference to the bee-line men made for Melanie once they set eyes on her.

Those same eyes, when they alighted on Liz, always moved straight on to the next object, for while her features were strong, even classic in their regularity, they also went unadorned, so nothing was made of them. Her hair was soft and silky, but mouse-brown and dead straight as well as very fine – the one time she had had it permed she had emerged looking like a Bride of Frankenstein – so she wore it in a neat and tidy French pleat. Her skin was unblemished, she had a nice smile showing flawless teeth, and a pair of large, expressive eyes which were unfortunately of an indeterminate sludgy-greenish-brown, neither one thing nor the other. To top everything off, her face when in repose, had a melancholic cast. More than once she had been told to cheer up when she had not been feeling in the least sad, merely thoughtful.

Melanie's internal radar, always scanning for leverage, had summed all this up on first meeting in one comprehensive sweep, and from then on she had proceeded to use Liz shamelessly for her own ends, parading her triumphant success with men (banners flying, bands playing), past the empty rostrum of Liz's failure, always introducing her to the ones who flocked to the flat as "the lynch pin of our quartet; such a big, strong capable girl," when it would be: "Liz, be a dear and reach to the top of the wardrobe – I am nowhere near big enough to reach all the way up there …" or "Liz, darling, can you unscrew this? My little wrists just don't have your strength …" The men would offer at once, but the damage had been done, mostly to Liz's self-esteem, which was eventually brutally trampled to death when she overheard herself referred to sniggeringly as "Melanie's pet elephant". Fortunately, her career having by then taken off, she having been hired by BB&B, she lost no time in making the quartet a trio by setting up on her own.

It therefore came as an anything but a pleasant surprise, more than six years later, to have Melanie cross her path again, this time as the *L'amoreuse* girl. Not having got anywhere as an actress – mainly, in Liz's opinion, because she had no talent – at yet another fruitless audition she had been approached by a scout for a model agency and become a highly successful and famous photographer's model, celebrated in gossip columns and glossy magazines alongside Linda Evangelista, Cindy Crawford and Claudia Schiffer, though she did no runway work, being neither tall enough nor androgenous enough. Melanie was all female, someone whose face was her fortune because she photographed like a dream. But time did not stand still and she was already twenty-seven (though her official age was twenty-three), so when offered the lucrative chance to become the Face fronting an extensive, and expensive, advertising campaign for an internationally known French perfume house about to launch a brand new fragrance, she had grabbed at it with both hands.

She had also dusted off the old ploy of using Liz as her foil, especially when she found out that Liz not only worked at the agency handling the account but had written the copy for the ads. Full of herself, and never anything less than difficult, Melanie had not hesitated to throw her weight around, only to find to her dismay that "our Miss Everett" still weighed a great deal more than she did. Worse, she was even more highly prized. Photogenic beauties, John Brittan told her bluntly, were a dime a dozen; copy-writers of Liz's talent and flair were rare and therefore highly valued. Not a man to put up with tantrums from anyone who thought themselves indispensable, he put the frighteners on Melanie good and proper and she, having her own best interests at heart – and mind, soul or anywhere else she could cram them in – had subsided, but only to bide her time.

Once the advertising campaign proved to be incredibly successful, increasing sales by some 60 per cent, she proceeded to appropriate all the credit and, as John Brittan was out of the way in Australia, had made life hell for the account executive appointed to be her minder. By then, as insurance, she had made sure of the head of the French

16

company, soon in total thrall, and at the slightest sign of opposition to her plans, threw a tantrum and threatened to quit.

Now that Liz was back, she felt her position to be unassailable to the point where she could say and do as she liked, especially with a woman who had never been any sort of opposition, no matter how good she was with words. Besides, she had to be paid back because John Brittan held her in such high esteem. Melanie did not like being beaten into second place, especially as, in her opinion, it was not Liz's slogan that had sold the perfume but Melanie Howard's face.

For her part, Liz had heard enough through the grapevine, which had tendrils long enough to reach Australia, to feel no surprise at being sought out for a little more of the same. What did surprise her was what Bertie had said about the new Creative Director being brought in specifically to handle Little Miss Superstar. From what Liz had heard he would have his work cut out. Not that Melanie's tantrums ever seemed to make any difference to the men who pursued her, like moths to a hypnotising flame. Smiling to herself, Liz mused sardonically: and here's me can't attract so much as a cabbage white!

She had a great sense of humour as well as the capacity to laugh at herself, and she used her quick tongue and gift for verbal fencing as weapons with which to parry the unthinking bludgeon of male indifference, which tended to refer to her as "Liz Everett? Oh, a good bloke!" It was either that or cry. Behind her unadorned face was a warm heart and a sterling character, but nobody – no man – had ever been sufficiently interested to see what lay underneath the plain brown paper wrapping which, since she was riddled with insecurities as a woman, she had never yet found the courage to discard.

"So? How is our resident brain?" Melanie taunted.

"I don't know. How is he?"

"Oh, come off it! You know very well that they call me Beauty and you—" Liz looked up and her expression had Melanie changing tack immediately. "I don't understand you," she prevaricated, understanding only too well. "Why don't you do something with yourself?"

"Like what? Grevious bodily harm?"

Melanie, who had absolutely no sense of humour, stared. Her looks were the centre of her existence; not to be beautiful was to her a tragedy far worse than fire, flood or earthquake, not to mention war, yet Liz never gave any sign of it muttering that she had none. Of course, she was well-liked, popular even, but it was as one of the guys; the crowd that lunched together every day at Luigi's, the nearby *trattoria* where Melanie would not have been seen dead. She lunched at Daphne's or Alistair Little or San Lorenzo, always at someone else's expense. At Luigi's, Liz always paid for herself, as they all did.

"Oh, well," Melanie shrugged with dismissive cruelty, "I suppose it would be too much to have brains *and* beauty. I've never found the need for brains myself. When you look like I do, who needs them? And men don't like clever women, anyway."

"Only those who feel intimidated by them."

"You won't say that about Tom Carey. He's got brains and then some." Her voice curled at the edges. "He is also devastatingly attractive … very American. He's taking me to lunch – he always does when I come to the Agency."

"Good for you," Liz said politely.

"I intend to knock him dead."

"Won't that rather defeat the object?"

Melanie looked blank.

"Never mind," Liz said. "Run along and make yourself even more beautiful. I can't wait to see the effect. I don't doubt for a moment that it will be devastating."

Melanie released her frustration by slamming the door behind her. Oh, yes, Liz thought, as she returned to her slowly decreasing pile of work, one look at that face and they hold out their hands for the cuffs. One look at me and they deny everything. She shrugged on a laugh. She was able to after so long. Ah well, she thought philosophically, you have lived for twenty-eight years with a plain face atop a large body and you are stuck with them for the next forty-odd years, so be thankful for what you've got and remember that you can't have everything. As it is, you have a great deal …

Ostensibly the chief copy-writer of her creative group, she was also a talented artist who produced her own lay-outs and storyboards to accompany the copy she wrote. John Brittan allowed her a great deal of latitude, because in coming up with the goods time after time after time, she had been responsible for more than one household

20

slogan over the years. Since she was constantly being head-hunted on behalf of rival agencies, he more or less gave her a free hand in order to ensure that she continued to write the copy and sketch the storyboards for his agency rather than a competitor's. Liz was very good at what she did, possessing every confidence in her abilities. Where she failed – lacking any kind of confidence at all – was with men. She had never had a steady relationship with one in her life, her trouble being, she had finally decided after much soul searching, that she was just not good enough for the men she might want, but far too good for the men who might want her, the operative word being *might*.

If she had had a mother to offer her both advice and consolation, it could have been different, but she had died, suddenly and shockingly, of a stroke when Liz was eleven. Thus her formative years had been supervised by her father's elder sister, a childless widow of formidable size and intellect (all the Everetts were large in size and brain), brisk common-sense and absolutely no sensitivity to the emotional difficulties which terrorised teenagers. Since she herself had never been less than certain of anything in her life, she neither perceived nor understood Liz's painful bewilderment.

At seventeen she was taken, reluctantly, by her two brothers to her first Rugby Club dance. Dressed in what her aunt deemed suitable for a virginal seventeen year old – wincingly unsuitable for someone of Liz's height and build – she had won first prize as wallflower. There was no one to turn to, to offer consolation or advice, since her aunt would have dismissed her tearful disappointment with a brisk: 'You must get over this blighting shyness of yours, Elizabeth. It is of no use standing around like a great gawk and blushing when someone so much as looks at you. Talk to people, make yourself known. *I* always did so."

Her self-confidence, always a fragile plant, had not the necessary wherewithal to withstand her aunt's steam-rollering, so it was no different the second time, or the third. By the fifth blooming of that perfect wallflower Liz had accepted that something was very wrong and decided that it had to be her. Why else the total indifference on the part of men? Why else did their eyes move past her to the pretty girls in the far corner? She was too tall, too big. Unfeminine. Today's woman was slender, fragile. Look at what passed for perfection in the pages of fashion magazines. Liz was twice their size. Women were not meant to be built like a scrum half. But with a father who was a clone of Arnold Schwarzenegger, and whose genes had totally overwhelmed those of her slender, petite mother, she was doomed, she supposed fatalistically. At the age when self-esteem is a fragile plant, requiring careful and tender cultivation, her rejection by the opposite sex had dug it up by the roots, aided and abetted by her aunt's brisk tossing of it on the compost heap.

Her resultant self-hate had been reinforced by a tactless remark made by an undergraduate who, on asking her why she wore her hair like an old-style hospital Matron, answered his own question by clobbering her with: "But curls would not be you, would they? I mean, you are not very feminine, are you?" That had sunk its teeth right in, up to the gums.

At Somerville she had not been invited to a single May Ball, or been asked out by even one undergraduate. So she had retreated into herself, not difficult since she tended to both shyness and diffidence, and concentrated on work, becoming known as a *swot* and a *grind*, always good for a crafty crib or a beautifully lucid exposition of a problem, confirming her prowess by achieving a brilliant First with honours. Where brains were concerned Liz was wildly popular with men; they had trodden a path as deep as a grave to her door soliciting help. The other path, the one that led to them asking her out as an attractive female, remained as virginal as she was.

Whatever it was that attracted men to women – and how many hours had she spent trying to figure *that* one out – she obviously did not possess it. That particular fairy had refused an invitation to her christening.

It was not as though she did not get on with men either. She did. They laughed at her wit, poached shamelessly on her goodwill and soft heart, took advantage of her kindness and good nature, treated her as one of the gang, a good sport, but never, ever asked her out. In the battle of the sexes she was always well behind the lines. When, in her senior year, she actually was asked out it was as a make-shift to complete a foursome, since one of the girls had gone down with measles caught from her youngest brother. Liz was the only girl available at short notice – Liz was *always* available. The man had been nothing special, but he was the first one she had ever been out with, so her innate shyness was made worse by her nervous uncertainty. This had led to her utter devastation when, on retiring from the loo that sixty seconds too soon, she had heard the others discussing how they could ditch her and go off as a threesome; the two men and the pretty girl they both wanted.

After scraping her ego up from the floor Liz had retired from the battlefield of the sex war, deciding that if she could not join them she would beat them – at what she was good at. Her work. Men had made it plain they had no use for the mountain. She would see what they made of Mohammed.

At twenty-eight love, to Liz, was something that happened to other people. The male-to-female ratio at the agency was roughly sixty-forty, and some 50% of that was constantly embarking and disembarking on the cruise liner S.S LOVE. Liz only ever got as far as the quayside to wave them off. And it was not, she reflected wistfully, as if she could not afford the fare, not with the high salary she was paid. But it was for doubles only, and it seemed she was condemned to be a "single, please," all her life.

Just then her internal telephone rang.

"Liz Everett here," she said crisply into the receiver.

"Good morning, Miss Everett, welcome back. My name is Tom Carey. No doubt you know by now that I am handling your accounts. I wonder, once you have got yourself settled in again, could we get together some time today? I should like to talk about things in general, but in particular *L'amoreuse*. Would three o'clock this afternoon be convenient?"

"It would," Liz answered promptly.

"Fine. My office at three, then."

He rang off. Lovely voice, Liz thought. Dark brown. And a nice accent. But what about the rest of him? In the light of that Mila Frey ad I think it would be as well if I found out ...

Her group always had the same table at Luigi's; the long one in the alcove away from the main restaurant. Over veal *parmigiano*, Liz exchanged gossip: hers about the new branch in Sydney, theirs about the new Creative Director.

She learned that he had so far made no waves, and was handling Melanie beautifully. "In the way she prefers to be handled

– in bed," was the general male consensus. "Because he allows her to flaunt him like mad," that of the female.

"They make a lovely couple," someone added facetiously.

"He's not married, then?" Liz asked, showing her inexperience.

"Not that we know of, but he is American, and you know how they are. He could be paying alimony to three ex-wives for all we know. I mean, he is awfully attractive," sighed Lucinda Rivett, who worked in the art department. "If they wanted him to handle me I'd be only too happy to let him."

"So he is young?" Liz was surprised. She had thought he would be of the same generation as John Brittan. Melanie had a thing about older men. Like the fact that they usually had more money.

"Same age as me," Bob Craven said. "Thirty-seven next birthday."

"Oh", said Liz. She had never had a young – well, youngish – Creative Director before. They had all been in their forties or more and much married and/or divorced. Hopefully, with any luck this one would not be any trouble either. Most of the others, once they had her measure, had left well enough alone, concentrating on the weak links in their chain of command and building their power bases. All the same, she thought, remembering that ad and knowing "Uncle" Fred Barnes only too well, she deemed it proper to ask, "But what about his other job – the advertising side of it. Does he know what he is about?"

"Oh, he's not just a handsome face," Bertie Fry assured her. "Lots of experience on some very high-powered accounts in the States; the ones with tens of millions in billing. Uncle Fred is no fool when it comes to hiring and firing. When are you seeing our American friend, by the way? He's already had us all in for a pep talk. Says he believes in getting to know the people he will be working with."

"This afternoon. Three o'clock."

"No love in this afternoon, then." Steve Ashton grinned snidely. "Normally when he lunches Melanie we don't see him till after four."

"Ah, but this *is* 'our Miss Everett'," Bertie admonished, "who, like me, has seen Creative Directors come and Creative Directors go. Which makes us both somewhat unimpressed by new brooms. I don't think we need worry about Mr Thomas

Carey too much, Melanie or no Melanie. I say let him enjoy it – and her – while he can." Paternally fond – and proud – of Liz, Bertie finished confidently, "Never fear, Liz. Take it from me, where Tom Carey is concerned you have absolutely nothing to worry about."

# Two

But Bertie Fry could not have been more wrong. One look at Tom Carey and Liz knew that he was trouble with a Capital 'T' because he fitted to the last detail her job description of 'Mr Right'. Rising to his feet he unleashed a laser of a smile before coming round from behind his desk to shake hands. No one looking at her reserved self-possession would have dreamed that behind it Liz was being assaulted by the most powerful sexual charge she had ever experienced.

He was tall – a good head taller than her – and solidly built yet slender, with dirty-blond hair and a cool, appraising pair of vivid blue-green eyes. His shoulders were broad, his hips narrow, his legs long. He reminded her of no one so much as Steve McQueen in one of her favourite movies: *The Thomas Crown Affair*.

Uncle Fred knew what he was doing, all

right, Liz thought dazedly. Melanie must have taken one look and cried, "Daddy, buy me that!" but Liz was also instantly aware of what had clinched it for Fred Barnes. Tom Carey had both authority and presence in large measure.

As she sat down in the chair opposite his desk, she saw that he had all her previous campaigns – texts and story-boards – laid out on his large desk, ending with the one she had worked on before leaving for Australia: the newest canned beer.

Tapping them with one long finger he said, "You live up to your reputation. These are remarkable in the way they catch the essence of the product. How do you do it? Where do you get your ideas from?" He sounded not only curious but deeply and genuinely interested. But Liz was ever cautious.

"Well … I think a lot about the product first: it's virtues, its selling points, its difference from whatever else is on the market, then I progress to what we have to get across to the public about those virtues. After that I fool around with some ideas, sketch them out. When one gels, says, *take me*, I make up a first presentation. If the account director likes it, we progress upwards to the creative head – now you."

When he smiled so did his eyes. "So you are an *Alice* fan too ..."

Liz felt a jolt of surprise. *Alice in Wonderland* was a book which held a special magic for her, but she had not met many men who felt the same, and never one who had spotted her allusion so quickly.

"I must have read it a dozen times," he went on. "You read a great deal, don't you?"

"Does it show?"

"Yes. You have a nice turn of phrase: sharp, witty, original. I see why you survived so many account directors." Tilting his chair back he regarded her thoughtfully. Liz made herself sit tranquilly under his appraising gaze. Finally, he said, "Your beer slogan slant is a very different one from the one they used in Australia."

"Different culture," Liz pointed out succinctly.

"True. And on the subject of culture, did you go to the opera house?"

"Yes. Several times."

"Are you an opera buff?"

"I like music in general."

"What else do you like?"

Wondering where this was leading, Liz answered, "Cooking. I like good food."

"Yes, that came through in the copy you wrote for the pasta sauce campaign. Something else we have in common. Italian is my favourite too. *Prosciutto* and *Osso Bucco* and *Lasagne* and *Risotto al Primavera* ... Do you know Italy?"

"I've been there several times."

"I thought so ... that also came through in your copy."

"We are what we write," Liz said lightly.

"So I've noticed." Then he changed tack. "And *L'amoreuse*; not just the perfume but the new make-up range they are bringing out. Any thoughts on that?"

"Should I have?" Liz asked carefully. She did not want to have to work on anything which brought her into contact with Melanie.

"Well, I am hoping you will do for the make-up what you did for the perfume."

"I only wrote the slogan—"

"But a great one. *'When l'amour is lacking, lure him with L'amoreuse'.*"

"It also had Melanie. Her face helped no end."

That brought no discernible reaction. Instead he asked, "What is your opinion of the perfume itself?"

"Distilled essence of sex."

"That's probably why women wear it. Do you?"

"No."

"Why not?"

"I don't wear any kind of perfume."

Again he regarded her at some length. "Yet you hit the spot with your slogan, which is no doubt why Francois Jourdain is keen for you to work your magic on his new range. He has asked me to make sure that you do."

Liz was equally determined to see that she didn't; she was not prepared to be Melanie's whipping girl, but all she said, non-committally, was, "I don't really know anything about it yet. I was in Australia when we got the account."

"Well, it is a case of early days yet, but we will definitely be using Melanie as the face of the campaign."

"Of course. Women have come to identify with her. She looks like a dream and that, after all, is what women are buying when they pay a fortune for a tiny bottle of fragrance."

"Is that why you don't wear it? You don't buy dreams?"

"I am a practical person. Dreams don't wear very well."

Again she managed to hold his probing gaze but he said nothing more and turned the conversation to her other accounts. This enabled her to relax, since when she was in command of a subject she had plenty of confidence. Besides, he was effortlessly easy to talk to, so much so that she was astounded when his intercom buzzed and she took the opportunity to check her watch, to find they had been talking for an hour.

"I'm sorry," she said, rising to her feet. "I tend to get carried away ..."

"No need to apologise. You talk like you write. Wittily and well. I only wish I had more time. Go ahead along the lines we discussed and we'll have another meeting at a later date. In the meantime, keep up the good work. I intend to give you a run for your money."

*For you, I'd run a marathon,* Liz thought, as she walked back to her office, envying Melanie from the depths of her soul. Not only was he awash with sexual charisma, he was highly intelligent, well-read – they had shared a taste in books – and well-travelled. The one thing she found she did not like was his selling of that sexuality to keep in line a woman whose ego and vanity demanded feeding on the hour every hour. But that rumour, she reminded herself firmly, is growing on the office grapevine, and you know how sour that fruit can be. If he was brought in to handle Melanie it could be because he is obviously up to the job of deflecting her demands. She couldn't imagine 'Uncle' Fred acting as Melanie's pimp. He was as old fashioned as they came. Nor could she imagine Tom Carey selling his sexual skills, considerable though her feminine instincts told her they must be. All right, so the *L'amoreuse* account was their biggest and most lucrative. Naturally the Three Wise Men don't want to lose it. But to buy its major selling point a stud to keep her happy … ? No way. They were gentlemen of the old school. If he was sleeping with her it was because he wanted to and for no other reason. At least she knew she should give him the benefit of the doubt. One meeting does not a prosecution case make.

But when Liz got home that night, she did something she rarely did. She examined her face and naked body in the full-length mirror behind her bathroom door. Was she going wrong in refusing to buy the dream? Was she wrong in saying baldly, *Look, this is how I am. No beauty. Take me or leave me.* Was that why they did leave her – on the shelf?

Later, in bed, she pondered her situation. If she was told to prepare a campaign to sell Elizabeth Everett, how would she go about it? Which salient points would she emphasize? How could she convince men that she was worth trying? Well, for a start, since she had no value as a purely decorative object she would have to concentrate on the functional aspect. She was intelligent, capable: she could write, draw; she could fit a plug, mend a fuse. She was an excellent cook, a good driver, played a winning game of scrabble. But you could hire cooks, electricians, drivers. What she needed to do was get men to see behind the plain-Jane externals to the Liz Everett who lived behind them, and since not one of them had so far been inclined to do so it had to mean that her self-presentation was not selling the product.

She mulled over it all next day, and then, at lunch on the following one, when she met her closest friend Jilly Markham she decided to take a second – expert – opinion.

"Jilly, tell me something – and honesty is what I'm after, no pulling of punches, please – what can I do to improve the way I look?"

Jilly, who had known Liz since they first worked together on one of Liz's earliest accounts asked, "What brought this on? I thought you had given up on your appearance."

"Never mind that. Just tell me. Am I totally irredeemable?"

Jilly sighed. "I have told you this before. You are not pretty and never will be. Your face is too strong. You have a good bone structure, but you just leave it lying, you don't do anything to enhance it. How many times have I asked you to let me loose with my paintbox? I could work wonders. They may call me a *visagiste* but that's only a fancy French title for make-up girl, and I have made up women with faces nobody would look at once, never mind twice, without my clever little tricks; women who are, in fact, nothing more *than* their make-up. All *you* need is enhancement. Combined with your presence – no, I do *not* mean your size – you could be something well worth any man's second glance, but you've got this blank space where your self-confidence should be, convinced you are Dracula's daughter constructed on a frame that went out with the dinosaurs. If you would only let me loose with my paints and powders …

Why haven't you ever? I've asked you often enough."

"I tried it once … and it failed – miserably."

"Probably because you did it all wrong, tried to make yourself into what you are not." At Liz's expression, she exclaimed, "I knew it! Probably wore your hair in curls as well as all the wrong colours." Not according to Aunt Louise, Liz thought. "You are striking, Liz, not pretty," Jilly went on. "A young Lauren Bacall, not a Goldie Hawn. Why don't you let me give you a complete make-over? It would do you the world of good. Your ego is pretty deflated right now, isn't it?"

"Does it show?"

"This is Jilly, remember? I am well acquainted with both you and your king-sized inferiority complex." Jilly faced her friend. "Who is he?"

"What makes you think—"

"Come off it," Jilly interrupted. "I happen to deal in women's faces, and the driving force behind the wish of every one of them to look as good as they can is some man. Why should you be any different? Though I am quite aware that you have been trying to be so for years. Mother Nature will not be thwarted, my dear Liz, in spite of the feminists. Next to self-preservation the mating instinct is the strongest we have. I am no Elizabeth Taylor but I do very nicely, thank you."

"You are very pretty – and not a monolith."

"Rubbish! Ninety years ago your build was the fashionable ideal. Just because whippets are now in fashion is no reason to put all St Bernard's down!"

"Oh no? Let me tell you what I once heard a man say about me, and I quote: 'She may not have gone to a redbrick university but she certainly is built like one!' " Even now, so many years later, that scar was still tender.

"The world is full of crass and insensitive men," Jilly said dismissively, cursing them inwardly. "Don't think you are the only woman to be rejected. I have been dumped myself – twice – as you well know! The thing to do is get it all together and prove to this man and all the rest who have ignored you that they are dead wrong! Nothing succeeds like success."

"And nothing cramps your style more than failure."

"Why will you persist in knocking yourself

down? Another coating of plaster so that when somebody else does it lessens the pain? Who is he?" demanded Jilly. She had seen too many women hung up on some man not to recognise the signs, though it was the very first time Liz had exhibited them.

"A very attractive man who is in no way attracted to me."

"Then set out to make him take a second look! Do something, for heaven's sake!"

"Like what? A demolition job?"

"*Will you stop being so defeatist!* All you have to do is make something of yourself."

"Slighter and shorter is what I'd like."

"I draw the line at wielding an axe," Jill retorted, and they both laughed, releasing the tension.

Gently, because she knew how thin Liz's skin was, Jilly said, "You do tend to be somewhat obsessed with your size, you know."

"Because I hate it!" Liz exclaimed vehemently. "What is feminine about being five feet ten inches tall and built like a scrum half? Men have made it plainer than plain that while they are only too happy to have me in the line-up they are not interested in seeing me after the game."

41

Jilly sipped at her spritzer before asking, "Did it ever occur to you that it might not be just your size? You are not exactly light-weight in the brains department either, you know. You have a quick, sharp tongue and don't suffer fools gladly. Not all men are up to a woman like that. However, if you really are serious about doing something about your appearance, why don't you let me help you? Just to give you an idea of how much can be done with and to the human face? What have you got to lose?"

"The last of my illusions if it does not work."

"Oh, it will work. I've seen it happen too many times to doubt it. Go on, take the plunge. Throw away the sack-cloth and ashes; wear clothes that will bring out the best in you. The raw material is there; it just needs polishing. You will never get off that self-defeating treadmill until you try."

"I know," Liz admitted. "But I am afraid to … If I go under again, Jilly, it will be for the last time."

The bleakness of Liz's tone pierced Jilly's heart. How strange, she thought, that a girl so confident about her capabilities could be so painfully vulnerable and insecure about her identity as a woman. Well, we all have our hangups; wasn't even a stunner like Princess Di tortured by doubts? Which was what was wrong with Liz. She had absolutely no sense of self-worth, and unless she acquired some pronto she was going to end up stir-crazy.

"Thanks for the pep talk anyway," Liz was saying, as she signalled for the bill. "I know you mean well."

The next day, she sat in on the weekly conference about the general state of the accounts in her group, but the main purpose was to discuss *L'amoreuse*.

Tom Carey made it plain what was expected of his team. "The client wants a new, combined campaign featuring both the perfume and the make-up range – which he has decided to call by the same name. He wants us to put Melanie in some highly romantic settings, which means we have to get to work right away to find them. He also wants the storyline written around her. He is hoping women will identify with her as the personification of the make-up range, just as they did with the perfume, and buy it accordingly. What I have in mind is a series of six ninety-second commercials filmed with all the glamour that can be crammed into them."

"Will the slogan be kept?" somebody asked.

"It is the only thing that will be. But new copy will be needed." He looked at Liz. "I want a continuing storyline, something like the enormously successful Gold Blend campaign of a few years back. A mini-soap, in fact. That will be your job."

But Liz was far gone in thought, her mind on what Jilly had said yesterday. So deep in her musings was she that only when Bertie Fry nudged her did she snap back to the present to find everyone looking at her.

"What ... oh, sorry ... I was miles away."

"You have some particular exotic setting in mind for the commercials?"

"There are several possibilities," Liz dodged, feeling her way, not having heard a word.

"How about Morocco?" Bertie Fry asked, throwing Liz a lifebelt. "That's romantic, isn't it? Shades of handsome Arab Sheikhs and such ..."

"Not since Saddam Hussein," Tom said dryly. "Sheikhs are out!"

"The Caribbean would be better," Liz said, her quick mind grasping the offered help. "White sand, huge moon, the sound

44

of the surf … Melanie in a drift of white chiffon and a piano playing Chopin …"

"Barbara Cartland country," somebody murmured sniffily.

"With a Cartland-type story?" somebody else asked. "Virginal romantic misunderstandings played through six 'to be continued' episodes?"

"No," Liz said, knowing what was wanted now and getting into her stride. "What's to misunderstand about Melanie? If the story has to revolve around her and her beauty then naturally there must be a man. In fact, I think there must be two. What woman would not thrill to be fought over by two men? That is where the tension will come in; each ninety seconds ending in a cliffhanger."

"Attagirl," Bertie said to Liz in an underbreath.

"Thanks for the nudge," she breathed back.

Several ideas were then tossed back and forth as the meeting took fire, and after an hour's discussion the general upshot was that the copy would be written by Liz once her storyline had been approved by the client, after which they broke up on a high note. As they were leaving Tom Carey said

45

to Liz, "Can you spare me five minutes?"

"Of course."

As the door closed behind the others the conference room phone rang. It was for Tom. While he talked Liz wandered to the window. If I was the woman pursued by two men, how would I react? she pondered, beginning to imagine settings and situations, the kind of men they would be, what they had to offer ...

"Penny for them," Tom offered and she came to with a start for the second time to find him standing beside her. He smelled of something sharp and lemony.

"You pay me a lot more than a penny for them," Liz retorted cheerfully, moving away for safety's sake.

"But worth every one if your ideas this afternoon are anything to go by. Could you do a quick, rough storyline for me? I'm seeing Francois Jourdain in Paris this Friday and it would be a great help if I had something to give him."

"Well, it is only a preliminary idea, you understand, but I think something along the lines we discussed could be developed very satisfactorily. Something like this ..." Seizing a pencil and some drafting paper she rapidly sketched a story-board of the story's opening: the woman – Melanie – engaged in the preparations for her wedding a week hence.

After a few minutes Liz looked up from her rapid sketching to find him regarding her oddly. "I have heard of perfect marriages, but your knack of marrying words to pictures is as perfect a match as I've ever encountered."

"Ah, that is because I have long been married to my job," Liz returned cheerfully.

"And is that enough?"

Why did he want to know? she thought irritably. She shrugged it off. "If I don't work I don't eat, and I like my creature comforts such as the roof over my head and a television set and to keep my Siamese in salmon."

"Not a Cheshire cat?"

Liz shook her head. "Empress is foreign royalty."

Just then the door slammed open and Melanie erupted inwards. "Tom, you said – oh!" She halted, eyes narrowing. Liz was no threat but Melanie trusted no one, especially if they were female.

"It's all right," Liz said, seizing the opportunity to escape. "Our business is concluded." As she made to pick up her sketches Tom laid a hand on them, his brushing hers as he did so. Liz's stomach went into freefall. "Leave them," he said. "I shall show them to Francois. Preliminary or not, they will give him a very good idea of our proposed campaign and if I know him he will be as enthusiastic as I am."

"What campaign?" Melanie interrupted imperiously.

"All in good time," Tom said, putting the drawings in the folder he had brought with him.

Melanie pouted. "If it is to do with *L'amoreuse* then I ought to be in on everything. After all we are one and the same."

"To the public, yes," Tom agreed, "but the agency does the spadework which puts that idea into their heads, and before that becomes reality there is a lot of work to do. Once it has been done then you shall see the proposal in its finished form, not before, because it is *after* that you take centre stage."

He was equable but firm, and Liz was astonished to see Melanie acquiesce, probably because of his last two words. Clever, she thought admiringly. How well he already knows her. For which relief much thanks, she thought, as she went back to her office.

Melanie accompanied Tom to Paris that weekend. Of course, was Liz's reaction when she was told. On the Monday afternoon of their return he summoned Liz to his office to tell her jubilantly that Francis Jourdain was totally enthusiastic about the idea for the new campaign and had given the go-ahead. Most important of all, in his enthusiasm he had increased the budget by 25%. It was all systems go, and the deadline for the TV and cinema previewing of the first commercial was set for seven months hence, for the pre-Christmas high-sales season. He was lavish in his praise of Liz's work but she knew that Tom's presentation had to have been every bit as good. She had come to appreciate – among so many other things about him – that when he liked what you did he threw himself behind you one hundred per cent. It was when he did not that you had to watch out. As one luckless Account Head had discovered. What Liz found harder to take was his obviously one hundred and one per cent endorsement of Melanie. It just goes to show, she comforted herself, men are indeed suckers for a lovely face.

Six weeks later, having been working long hours at high pressure, Liz decided she needed a break. She had devised the slight but believable love story – which was easy since she was by now deep in the throes of her own romantic imaginings – converted it into copy and delivered her final, beautifully drawn and coloured presentation story-board, each picture under its transparent protective cover. If the client approved, then the campaign would move on to the second stage: the actual shooting of a series of six ninety-second segments by a company which specialised in such work, with a director who had been responsible for more than one prize-winning commercial and was hoping that this one would be his ticket to a Hollywood sound stage. Melanie's wardrobe was being specially designed, her *L'amoreuse* make-up from the House of Jourdain's newest range had been selected, and a *visagiste* from the Paris house would come to do her face before each shoot.

Several locations had been chosen by Tom, whom Liz found to have keen visual sense when it came to what would look good on camera, as well as what would, as he put it, "play". He was far and away the best Creative Director she had ever worked with. Nothing escaped his eagle eye, and he had come to be respected by everybody on the five floors occupied by Brittan, Barnes & Beckwith. Liz was now in no doubt whatsoever that it was not just because Melanie fancied him that he had been brought in to run the creative side of BB&B. She also gloried in the fact that he had made it plain he approved of the way she ran her department, which was why she had no qualms about asking if, now that her own job was done to his satisfaction, he could spare her to take a week's leave. He agreed at once, saying, "I am a great believer in recharging the batteries, and you must have drained yours with all your recent hard work. Going anywhere nice?"

"Paradise," Liz answered flippantly, not knowing where she was going, only that she felt the need to go.

"In that case may I come too?"

It was out of her mouth before she could stop it: "But I thought you went there all the time – with Melanie."

Why, oh why? did I say that, she keened to herself later. His face had taken on a coldness she felt in her bones, the eyes turning to icecubes she felt he had put down her back, causing her to shiver. I need this break, she told herself, as she packed that

51

night. Seeing the two of them together these past weeks – for Melanie had made it her business to make it clear to all and sundry that he was *her* property – had been chafing at Liz's sensibilities. But who would think, looking at me, that I had any? she derided herself. The trouble was that as time went on and she became even more inextricably caught on the hook of Tom Carey's powerful attraction for her, she found it increasingly difficult to respond naturally to him. Now her stupid – and jealous, she realised – remark had gone and ruined everything. Theirs was no more than a working relationship, no matter what her inner longings might be, but as they went it was the best she had ever had. Now she had gone and put both feet right through it. Idiot! she berated herself. Next morning, after a night spent in fruitless recrimination, she gave her Siamese into the temporary care of her neighbour in the basement flat, with whom Empress shared her affections. As she got into the Golf she had bought with her last Christmas bonus she had no clear idea of a destination, only that she did not want to go home. A year ago her father had retired as senior partner of the firm of Consulting Engineers he had run for thirty-five years, sold the big house in Wimbledon and moved with his sister to the cottage he had bought in the small Suffolk village where they had both been born. It had a large garden he could contentedly work in for hours, while his sister could bring her organisational talents to bear on the various village events.

That at twenty-eight, unlike her elder brothers, Liz showed no signs of marrying did not worry her father. He had always been a liberal in his attitude to his children, into whose lives he never pried. His sister did not approve, but Liz had always known that whatever she wanted to do was all right with her father as long as she was happy, and they had never lived in each other's pockets anyway.

So once she left London she turned the car West. It was not a part of the country she knew well, never having been further than Torquay, where the family had taken holidays twenty years before. She would just drive until she saw some place which said "Stop". Who knew where she might end up? Truth to tell she did not particularly care. Just so long as they were pastures new.

# Three

The evening of her second day found her deep into southern Cornwall, having left Truro at lunch time and taken the minor roads, avoiding the A394 that would have taken her to Penzance. Instead she wandered down to Falmouth, past Rosemullion Head and up towards Helford Passage, where, as it was dinner time and she was hungry, she stopped at a small, pleasant looking pub-come-inn on a headland overlooking a steep-sided valley giving lovely views of the Helford River. It was inviting enough to impel her inside to ask if they had a room. They had, so she booked in, ate a solitary dinner and then decided to walk off her restlessness. She had been driving all day, and apart from needing to stretch her legs, she wanted to tire herself out so as to be able to sleep, thus shutting down the treadmill of her thoughts, which these days revolved endlessly around Tom Carey. It was a lost cause, Liz knew, but she could not help it. Working with him, seeing him at least once every day only increased her envy of Melanie, her day-dreaming of a situation where the positions were reversed and her frustration at not being able to do anything about it; worse, her self-disgust at her own cowardice at being afraid to try.

Ironically, it was a lovers' night. A big moon, a silvered, cloudless sky – no doubt the reason why the river, some two hundred feet below, glittered like silver lamé – and a breeze as soft as a lover's breath. Deep in thought, she walked slowly and aimlessly. It was not until she was almost on it that she saw the house, heard the music, realised she had somehow blundered onto private property, unseeingly deviating from the cliff path and taking another which wound down the sloping cliffs to a secluded little bay, rendered invisible from the clifftop by a heavy growth of tall rhododendron bushes.

Two-thirds of the way down the slope, on a plateau that erosion had carved into the cliffs, someone had sited a small but beautiful house, white as sugar icing under the moonlight, presiding over an equally small but perfect Italian formal garden, filled with flower beds, marble statuary and fountains. She could smell honeysuckle, overlaid with the heavier sweetness of roses and the spice of herbs: rosemary, sage, borage and lime, while over it all, hanging on the night air, a glorious mezzo-soprano voice was singing with lyrical joy what Liz – a passionate lover of music – recognised as one of the *Songs of the Auvergne*; the one called *Bailero*. She took root. Open mouthed she stared into a fairy tale.

Eventually, as if magnetised, she was drawn further down the path, which widened as it descended, and found herself in the gardens proper. There was no one about, and the house showed no lights. Whoever owned it was sitting in darkness listening to their CD player. Coming to a marble bench, Liz groped for it and sat down, wholly caught by the mood of the night, the beauty of her surroundings and that glorious voice, one she did not recognise, though she knew she would never - forget it. Closing her eyes she let it all wash over her, allowing it to fill her own deep pool of emotional longing until it overflowed in tears. Hot, scalding, they welled from her closed eyes to run silently down her face and drip from her chin onto her folded hands. She sat that way until the music ended, its last note fading slowly. It was then, as the silence held its breath, that a sob tore from the very heart of her, like a piece of flesh wrenched away with red-hot pincers, so that it came out as a gasp of pain.

"Who is there?" demanded a strong, resonant voice. "Someone is there. Who is it?"

In sudden panic Liz rose to flee, hastily smearing her wet face with the backs of her hands, unwilling to be caught with her emotions on display.

"Wait!" The voice was commanding, so imperative that in spite of herself she paused, turning to see who had issued the order. Coming towards her was a man, a white stick held – but not being used, she noted – in one hand. He knew where he walked. As he neared her she saw he was no longer young yet had a still strikingly hand-some face under a mane of iron-grey hair. He did not wear dark glasses, and in the bright light of the moon his eyes glittered like jet even though they saw nothing. "Don't run away," he commanded, but not so authoritatively, sensing she had stopped.

As he came right up to her Liz broke into

a hasty apology: "I'm sorry. I didn't mean to trespass ... I wasn't aware that I had until I heard the music and saw the house ... I was convinced I had strayed into a fairy tale ..."

He chuckled. "I am no ogre, I assure you, but I am glad you like my house. Might I know with whom I have the pleasure of sharing what seem to be mutual interests?" he asked humorously.

"My name is Elizabeth Everett. I am staying at the inn back there ..." Forgetting he could not see, for there was nothing of a blind man about him, Liz gestured behind her. "I came out for an after dinner stroll but somehow – and I am still not sure how – I found myself here, saw the house, heard the music and – was caught. I apologise for the intrusion. It was not meant."

"No need." He dismissed that with an expressive gesture. "I am pleased and flattered that you appreciate both."

"A Palladian villa was the last thing I expected to find in Cornwall ..." Liz snapped her fingers. "Of course! I thought it seemed familiar ... now I remember! The Villa Paradiso north of Vincenza ... that is where I saw it before."

There was a smile in his voice as well as

58

on his face. "You have indeed. My father was Italian, my mother Cornish, and when circumstances forced me to return to live in my native country I decided I would live in a house copied from my adopted one, so I had a replica built, stone for stone, but half the size. This small plateau would not accommodate anything like the size of the original."

That meant money, Liz thought, studying his face, as vaguely familiar as his house. "Should I know you?" she asked tentatively. "I feel I should ... are you famous?"

"I was once."

"Were you an actor? I seem to recognise your face ..."

"What I did required acting, yes." In his amusement his voice took on a timbre that identified him for her.

"Of course I know you! Well, your voice anyway. You are John diMarco."

"I am indeed."

"Well, this is turning out to be a night of nights! I have most of your CDs at home. The thinking girl's *Don Giovanni*."

His laugh was one of delight. "Nicely put," he praised, "since that is exactly what I tried to be."

"Well, it was your most famous role.

Those who are supposed to know said you were the best Don ever."

"I was." It was said with no false modesty. "But now, the only singing I do is in a recording studio. It is six years since I was on stage".

"I knew you had retired, but not to this miniature paradise."

"Not many people do."

"Then I will leave you to it, with apologies for my inadvertent intrusion."

"No … please … do not run away." He put out a restraining hand. "I welcome your presence. I suspect that you took the wrong path. It divides at the top of the hill; one way continues along the clifftop, the other comes down here, but there is a gate, which is normally closed."

"I did not see a gate … but I was so deep in thought I did not see anything. I was just wandering."

"A lost sheep," he teased. When she did not answer he went on: "And what are you doing in Cornwall? Taking a holiday?"

"A break from work."

"Alone?"

Liz nodded, forgetting he could not see before saying a brief, "Yes."

"And where have you come from?"

60

"London. I live and work there."

"And what is your work?"

"I am an advertising copywriter."

"And do you write well?"

"Yes, I do."

"Good for you. I like people who have confidence in themselves. I always did." Just then, a gong sounded sonorously, emanating from the house. "Ah … Adelina summons me for my nightcap. Might an old man invite a young woman to share it with him?"

Liz hesitated. She was bemused by his charm, captivated by his charisma, and from the start been conscious of an instant *rapport*, but nevertheless her innate shyness asserted itself.

"Please," he urged. "I will show you my house, and thus see it again through your eyes."

That did it. "In that case …"

"Excellent! Kindred spirits are rare, but I think we have discovered one in each other. That you were caught by the night, the music and my house tells me so. Come, let me show you some more of its beauty."

She followed him as he unerringly led the way down gravelled paths and past a marble fountain from which a statue of a nymph poured water from an urn. He went confidently up the first flight of shallow stone steps to the lower of two terraces, then up the second flight to the house itself. Lights had been switched on, and through doorlike windows she could see a richly furnished interior. Following him in, she found herself in a jewel of a two-storeyed hall which ran from the front to the back of the house: frescoed walls, velvet hangings, superb painted and gilded furniture, gleaming marble floor, grand staircase and glowing rugs. Going to a massive fireplace he tugged at the tapestry bell-pull hanging beside it before leading the way through an open door into a smaller, but also richly furnished room.

"Sit down, sit down," he urged, waving a hand rich with *largesse*. Liz did so, and at that moment a woman followed them in, carrying a silver tray on which were placed a decanter and glass. No longer young, she was tall, like Liz, big, like Liz, but with all the confident assurance Liz lacked. Blackhaired, though greying at the temples, oliveskinned, dark-eyed, she moved with the consummate grace and regality of one who knew she was a queen.

"Ah ... Adelina, another glass if you

please. We have an unexpected guest. This is Elizabeth Everett, who strayed into the garden and stayed to listen to you singing."

"It was you singing?" Liz asked in surprise, as Adelina made to go.

"A recording Adelina made some years ago," the Don explained.

"It was beautiful. You have a glorious voice."

"*Grazie, signorina*," Adelina murmured on a smile, but her black-olive glance was penetrating and missed nothing. Satisfied, she set the tray on the trolley at the side of the throne-like chair in which Liz's host had seated himself, then exited as silently as she entered.

"Adelina is my housekeeper," John diMarco said, the smile in his voice making it clear he was fully aware of the impact she had made.

She was back within seconds, carrying another tray and a second glass which she placed by the decanter before leaving them alone, closing the door behind her. Liz was wondering if she ought to offer to pour then was glad she didn't when she saw how expertly he reached for the decanter to half-fill the two smallish glasses with what she surmised was brandy from its colour. Then he lifted one and she only had to put out a hand to take it.

"How do you do it?" she asked, fascinated.

"I can hear you breathe. My hearing has – of necessity – become acute." Reaching to the silver box by the decanter he lifted its lid to extract a long, thin cheroot. "Now that I no longer have to be so concerned about nightly performances and the state of my throat I allow myself one of these with my glass of brandy on special occasions. Tonight I regard as such an occasion. One reaches out for unexpected pleasures even as one accepts the expected pain." He lit his cheroot, blew smoke pleasurably.

"How long have you been blind?"

"Six years. I was injured during an open-air performance of *Don Giovanni* in Verona. In the statue scene, I fell awkwardly and hit my head. There were no immediate ill effects but it turned out that I had somehow damaged the optic nerve which, slowly but surely, ceased to function, and over a period of time I lost my sight. I was fortunate that it took a little more than a year, so I was able to plan and build my house."

"You planned well," Liz complimented feelingly. "This really is paradise."

His smile was indulgent. "To you, perhaps, but I have been there and I can tell you it is nothing like this."

Liz found herself smiling in return. "How lucky you are! Had I been fortunate enough to visit paradise I doubt I should have come back to tell the tale."

She sipped her brandy. It was like silk; she felt it sliding through her veins, warming and relaxing. What a marvellous old man, except that there was nothing old about him. In his fifties? she hazarded. He had retired in his prime at a relatively young age. Yes, early fifties, she decided, and was astonished when, seeming to read her thoughts he asked, "How old are you?"

"Twenty-eight."

"Ah … young. I am thirty years older than you."

"You don't look it."

"No. I never looked my age. When I was young I looked older. I was still singing the Don at fifty – and playing him too."

Again there was that subtle amusement in his voice. He was paying her the compliment of treating her as a woman of the world, while in no way being offensive. She had the feeling that he was the last man in the world to call a spade a digging implement, but since she herself had no use for the current mealy-mouthed hypocrisy of political correctness she was both glad and grateful. Remembering what she knew about him – mostly from the information in the programme notes of her CDs, and a biography she had read a few years ago, he had been a *Don Juan* in life as well as in his art. His amatory exploits had been legendary, and he had left a trail of adoring women from Stuttgart to San Fransisco. He was a handsome older man; he must have been devastating when he was younger. The illustrations in the biography had shown a virile, black-haired man of devilish handsomeness. Men who photographed like that were even better in real life. Liz wondered how Tom Carey photographed.

Wrenching her mind away from that dead-end she asked, "Tell me about Adelina. With a voice like that she must have been a professional too."

"A very fine mezzo-soprano, as you have heard. She was my mistress and she gave up her own career to come with me into retirement. Now we live together in this place in peace and contentment. And you – do you have a lover?"

Utterly taken aback by his uncompromising directness, Liz gulped before managing a short, "No."

"Why not? I thought, in this sexually obsessed day and age, a woman without a lover – lovers – is like a cat without a tail: most unusual."

"Then I am unusual."

"I have already come to that conclusion. You have a lovely voice – a contralto. Do you sing?"

"Only in the bath."

"And do you look as you sound?"

"No."

"Ah." He said no more on that subject but turned the conversation to other things. When the clock, a delicate thing of porcelain and ormulu, struck the hour, Liz was astounded to see it was eleven o'clock.

"Heavens! I had no idea it was so late ... I have kept you up. I am so sorry."

"No, no ... the time has flown because we enjoy each other's company. And since we have never stopped talking you have still not seen my house, in which case you must come to lunch tomorrow, then I can show you round at leisure. Shall we say one o'clock?"

"Oh, but ... I don't want to make a nuisance of myself."

"Nonsense! You amuse and intrigue. I do not know when I have enjoyed conversation more. Please, indulge an old man and come to lunch tomorrow so we may engage in further talk."

Unused to being the object of a man's charm, skilfully used with both purpose and intent, Liz could feel the pull he was exerting. He was a charmer all right. Besides, where else had she to go?

"I should like that very much."

"Excellent. One o'clock, then."

Setting her glass down on the tray, Liz said, "If I go back the way I came will I end up back at the inn?"

"Yes – the path to the right of the gate. If you find it open, please shut it behind you."

He had got to his feet, now he held out a hand. She took it and he ran his fingers over hers in a way that was both sensitive and appreciative. "Fine hands ... long, supple fingers, beautiful nails. Hands tell much. I have learned to see with mine. Would you allow me to see you?"

Liz found herself saying: "Of course."

She stood very still while he ran the tips of his fingers lightly across her brow, round her eye sockets, over her cheeks, down her nose, lightly across her mouth – where they lingered – rounding her jaw to her throat. "Such a passionate mouth," he murmured, dropping his hands to her shoulders. "You are tall, and broad shouldered – much like Adelina. She is magnificent too."

Liz reeled inwardly. Had she heard aright? He *had* said she was magnificent?

"No one has told you this before?" he asked shrewdly, reading her body stance under his sensitive hands.

"No ... never."

He said something in Italian that sounded like an imprecation, then in English, "What is it in this day and age that makes society regard a woman built like a woman as something to be ashamed of? Adelina tells me that the women of today still struggle to resemble nothing so much as stick-insects. *Basta!* Do men not recognise a goddess when they see one?"

Liz was open-mouthed with shock. First he said she was magnificent, now he was calling her a goddess! This from a famed connoisseur of women.

"I think I have surprised you," he said into her stunned silence.

"That is the understatement of this or any century," Liz managed in strangled tones. "The only way I ever saw myself as a

69

goddess was as a larger-then-life statue of one."

"Never! Not with that mouth. What colour is your hair?"

"Mouse."

"And your eyes?"

"A sort of muddy green."

"You disparage yourself. Why?"

In the face of his uncompromising directness she could only respond in kind. "Because I have never been led to think of myself as other than plain as a pikestaff."

"Led by whom – men?"

Liz was silent. He had brought back all she had managed to forget in the past couple of hours, yet she was also aware that this incredibly intuitive and understanding man was somehow drawing an abscess of inner anguish that had been growing since the advent of Tom Carey.

And you know how, don't you, she lashed at herself. Because he is blind. Because he cannot look at you and let you see the indifference in his eyes. For a little while, believing his flattery, she had managed to forget her hangups, now it was as though he had thrown open a door to reveal a full-length mirror into which she looked at herself and recoiled.

"Come now ..." he said in a voice of such affinity that Liz felt her throat thicken and her eyes prick. "I think that what you are is raw material of much value. All you need is polishing and refining. Even a diamond has no sparkle until it is cut and polished; in its raw state the uninitiated would cast it aside as a worthless pebble. I think you need polishing. And that takes skilled hands. Take it from me, who has always been and always will be a lover of women and all they are, you are indeed magnificent. You stand superbly and your profile would do justice to another goddess – the Venus de Milo, a lady whose proportions do not fit into current standards either. You stand out, make no mistake. I cannot see you, but I have talked to you; you have a distinctive personality, a witty tongue, a keen mind. I think perhaps your – abundance – would be a great deal too much for many men because they would not be able to handle it, in which case I do not think they would be of much interest to you, am I right? I think you are a young woman with great potential but little faith in herself, which is why you were sitting in my garden weeping ... is that not so?"

Mortification swept over Liz in a drowning

wave. She had been listening to words of such honeyed sweetness that the bucket of cold water which followed them had her gasping.

"You are young, and youth is a time for happiness; a time to make one's mistakes and learn for one's future. The trouble is that youth does not possess the experience to deal with unhappiness; that, alas, comes with age. Is it a man? At your age it usually is."

"It is only an infatuation. I will get over it," Liz said flatly.

"He does not return your feelings, then?"

"He does not even know I have them."

"Ah … I see …"

Blind or not, Liz knew he did. This man "saw" more than people with twenty-twenty vision.

"Tell me," he asked next, "have you ever read Wilkie Collins' *The Moonstone*?"

Wondering what that had to do with anything, Liz replied, "Yes, a long time ago."

"Do you remember Rosanna Spearman, the poor servant girl and ex-thief, who fell in love at first sight with Franklin Blake, though he did not so much as look in her direction because he was never really aware of her existence?"

"Yes," Liz answered, after a moment's thought because she was stunned by his perceptiveness as to her own situation. "Now I do ..."

"She wanted desperately for him to see her as a living, breathing human being, but did not know how except by confronting him, which events conspired to prevent. So she killed herself. I do not think you are that far gone, but I would advise you to make your presence felt where your young man is concerned. If it has no effect then it is not meant to be. In this life, we cannot always have what we want. You will find someone else. A magnificent creature like you will not be left to mourn for long."

He had said it again! Was it – oh, God, could it possibly be – was she wrong? Could it be that she was, far from not being good enough, *far too much* for a great many men. She would far, far rather be that than not enough.

"I think I have given you a great deal to think about," he said shrewdly, into her ringing silence. "So go away and think about it and tomorrow we will talk some more."

"I would like that," agreed Liz dazedly. If he was going to say things such as he had said tonight she would listen to him forever. Never had she heard such emollient words, balm to a self-esteem that had been scraped raw. But more than that, his special brand of ointment contained an even more potent ingredient: hope.

He insisted on accompanying her to the top of the first flight of steps, where she saw that the gardens were lit, making her way back easy to find. He held out his hand and she took it, but instead of a handshake he raised hers to his lips, in a courtly gesture that was theatrical yet in no way a mere piece of acting.

"*Arriverderci*, until tomorrow ..."

# Four

Liz all but reeled back to the inn, feeling not only drunk on possibilities but as if she had just been given a brand new ninety-nine-year lease on life. Reaching the cliff-top path she saw that there was indeed a fence-like wooden gate and it was wide open, as her host had surmised. Closing it carefully behind her she saw that had it not been so she would have missed it because it was shrouded by masses of blood-red rhododendrons. God bless whoever left it open, she thought fervently, for had they not she would never have discovered that through it lay a magic kingdom. Had she dreamed it all? No – she could still taste the brandy, not to mention feel its intoxication. That fantastic house and garden and its even more magical owner were real. So were the things he had said to her. That she was magnificent! That she was a goddess!

She drifted back to the inn and up the

stairs, bidding the landlord an absent good-night. In her room she undressed, cleaned her teeth, but before climbing into bed she once again examined her naked self in the Edwardian pierglass that stood by the dressing table, only this time she did so in the light of John diMarco's amazing words, trying to see through her eyes what he had read through his fingertips. Yes, she was big, but not fat; just built on generous lines. Everything was in the right proportion, just not in the currently fashionable androgynous waif mode decreed by designers whose preferences were for waistless, flat-bottomed men anyway. Hers was unmistakably the body of a woman, not a boy.

That charismatic magician was right, she realised in stunned delight. Blinded by self-hatred she had been unable to see herself as anything other than the monolith a handful of crassly insensitive men had labelled her: men who, had she been confident of herself, she would have dismissed as third-raters. In allowing them to judge and condemn her, she had made a terrible mistake. Now, because of a blind old man she saw what they had not been able to: that she *was* magnificent. Full, high, firm breasts with not so much as a hint of droop; wide-hipped yes, and with a behind that was worthy of the name, but long-legged with it. Through his praise she saw not the unfashionably large female of her own self-loathing, but a woman of abundance. The irony was that it had taken a blind man to make her see it! Yes, there was a lot of her, in more ways than one, and it would take a lot of man to handle her. Like Tom Carey. He was handling Melanie, and she was a handful. Me, I'm two handsfull, Liz thought proudly.

What she had been trying to do, she realised belatedly, as she got into bed, was compete on other women's terms when she should have been competing on her own. Naturally she had failed, since she had been trying to be what she was not and never would be, and all because at a vulnerable age she had been steered wrong and allowed a few poor specimens of the opposite sex to tell her to get off the road.

She lay for a long time thinking, thinking, and found that a lot of wrong conclusions were now put right. Like the time a few years ago when Jilly had coaxed her to go to her one and only fancy dress party. The theme had been fictional characters and she had been persuaded to go as Carmen, with a black wig, full petticoated skirt, off the shoulder blouse, and bare legs and feet, her skin stained gypsy brown. Jilly had applied the same stain to her face, along with a bright scarlet lipstick, and when Liz had noticed more than one young man staring – a couple of them fixedly, their eyes following her round the room – she had at once thought it was because she was an object of ridicule, grotesque in her obviously all-wrong choice of costume. What if it had been because they were not only impressed but cowed by such abundance? Had they done no more than stare because that was all they were up to doing? Hang on a minute, she scolded herself roundly. You are letting a blind man's words run away with your imagination. This is not a case of From Nothing to Everything in One Fell Swoop. But they *had* stared. It had made her feel uncomfortable and larger than ever because her basement-level evaluation of herself had as usual taken it for condemnation rather than approbation. What if she were to take up Jilly's offer and put it to the test? It was the one way she could find out for absolutely sure. If she was to polish her raw material, unveil the goddess – what then? Would Tom Carey see her in a different light? As a woman, not a brain. It would be a risk, of course. She could be – that lover-of-women in his white-icing house could be – dead wrong. But if she was ever to get out from under, she had no choice but to take his advice and make the effort, make her *presence* felt. The thing to do was start now, while he was around to urge her on, filling her with the confidence she needed. When she fell asleep she was smiling.

Next morning, after breakfast, Liz drove into Falmouth, found a shop that sold her size and bought herself her very first pair of jeans and some cotton, figure-hugging tee shirts. No more knee-length overshirts. But a stubborn residue of doubt obviously lingered, because as she hesitated in front of the mirror in the changing room the saleslady said, "Is there something you don't like?"

Liz turned to her. "Tell me the truth," she requested. "Am I too big for jeans?"

The saleslady – no sylph herself – looked askance. " 'Course you're not! We stock up to size twenty! Mind you, that is a bit much, but sixteen isn't. You've got curves so why not show them off?"

"All right," Liz said, going for broke. "I'll take them – and the three tee shirts."

She kept the jeans and one of the tee shirts – the white one – on as she walked back to her car, acutely self-conscious at first, staring fixedly ahead, but soon jubilantly reassured by the reaction she got. For the first time in her life she was whistled at, by some men erecting scaffolding, while a window cleaner stopped what he was doing to watch her retreating figure out of sight, none of which she found in the least demeaning, only flattering. She was a bud in the early stages of flowering and needed lots of what she had lacked for so long: male approbation.

Back in her room, singing to herself, she hung away her tent dress, never to be worn again, then took out the pins and brushed out her hair, tying it back with the bright ribbon she had also acquired. On using the dark brown mascara the girl behind the beauty counter in Boots had recommended, she found that her lashes, given definition, turned out to be spider's legs, while the bright scarlet lipstick she had also bought gave her mouth instant recognition. She looked good! She actually looked good! So taken was she with her newly revealed self that she lost track of time and when she did look at her watch found she had less than five minutes to get to the villa. She fled.

He was sitting on the terrace when she leapt them, two at a time.

"No need to rush," he chided. "You are punctual."

"Only because I ran all the way."

"On those long legs I am sure that was no hardship. Come, sit down, get your breath back, although I must say that today, you sound – lighter. As though some great weight had been lifted."

"It has, thanks to what you told me last night. I think you might just have saved my life."

"Nonsense! I think that it is because you had been out in the cold for so long. Today the sun is shining, on you and in you; the flower has unfurled itself and bloomed at last."

"You know," Liz said after a moment, "for a blind man you see an awful lot."

"Since I have been blind I have learned that it is possible to perceive things the eyes miss. Now, a drink I think. Adelina has placed everything ready. What would you like? Something long and cold, perhaps. Campari and soda?"

"That would be perfect."

"While I make it, you will please tell me what you have done with yourself today: what has caused the flower to blossom?"

She did so, and when he handed her a tall, deeply pink, ice-clinking glassful, garnished with a thick slice of juicy orange, he said, "Obviously a successful expedition. The joy in your voice tells me so."

"It was, oh, it was! You have no idea ..." How could he, when she had not had the slightest inkling herself?

"Then let us drink to your continued blooming and the start, I hope, of an equally beautiful friendship."

Adelina came out to them, acknowledging Liz graciously before speaking in Italian to her host. He nodded, replying in the same language. When Adelina had gone: "She was asking if she should go easy on the garlic. I said no. Am I right?"

"Yes."

"Adelina is a superb cook. I guarantee you have never tasted anything like her pasta."

After her first mouthful of *fettuccine primavera* Liz said in reverent tones, "You are absolutely right. I haven't." The sauce was rich with cream, and contained young asparagus, tender celery, zucchini, pimiento and carrots, all sprinkled with freshly chopped parsley.

After the pasta they had veal, cooked in marsala, button mushrooms and sauté potatoes, with which they drank a white wine from John's own vineyard in Tuscany. They then had the lightest, frothiest *zabaglione*, and finished off with fresh fruit and cheese.

"Concerning paradise, I have to tell you that your house is well named," Liz groaned once she had managed to drag her full stomach to the swing on the terrace where coffee awaited them.

"Adelina will be pleased. She said you looked like a woman with an appreciation of the good things in life. Tell me what you are wearing today."

"Jeans and a tee shirt. Did Adelina tell you what I was wearing last night?"

"Some sort of a sack, she said. Something to hide under, and in a dark, miserable colour. She also said you arrived like a damp squib and went off like a sparkler."

Embarrassed as she was, Liz had to laugh. God knows it was true.

"But today you have taken off your shroud. Do I take it that you have decided to make your presence felt?"

"I am going to try. Thanks to your encouragement."

"So you no longer think your size is a liability?"

"After seeing Adelina – no."

"*Brava*! In my line of work I have met many generously proportioned women: Joan Sutherland, Jessye Norman, Montserrat Caballe. The great Callas was not always the sylph she became."

"Did you work with her?"

"Once, when I was a young singer making my way up the ladder, more than thirty years ago now."

"Would you tell me about your work? I should love to know what the world of opera is like."

With an indulgent smile he readily began to tell her of how he went about interpreting a role, once again holding her spellbound. It was obvious he liked to talk because he did it eloquently, entertainingly, occasionally scabrously, sometimes caustic and often profound. "But I have talked long enough. Come, now that our lunch is digesting nicely, I will give you a tour of my house."

He took her into every room but the private ones, showing her what he called "his treasures"; things he had acquired during his travels, some with an operatic history, some merely because he liked the look or feel of them. The operatic collection was all in one room and was mostly memorabilia. Costumes, wigs, props, photographs, even a portrait, of himself in his most famous role. Before this Liz lingered longest. Yes, he had been handsome: darkly and sensually compelling. Unconsciously, she sighed.

"Do I remind you of someone?"

"You look like no one I know," she replied truthfully, turning away to examine a costume. "These robes must have been awfully heavy to wear."

"Some. *Don Carlos*, and *Nabucco*. Not so much *Scarpia* or *Count Almaviva* or *Don Giovanni*. Men were the peacocks in their day, but the costumes of Mozart's heroines are also exquisite. I have some of them here – they were Adelina's. Would you like to see them?"

"Oh, please, I should love to."

When Adelina answered the summons of the bell, she smiled and agreed at once to the Don's request, going over to the big cupboard which lined one wall, opening folding doors to reveal a rackful of dresses.

"Oh, beautiful, beautiful ..." crooned Liz,

going over to stroke silk and velvet and encrusted lace.

"You put?" Adelina asked. "They will fit. We are the same – *misura* – how you say?"

"Size," said the Don, which was how Liz was now thinking of him.

"Yes, yes ... this one is very nice ... Countess Almaviva ..." It was of champagne satin with an underskirt of creamy lace.

"Are you sure?"

"Yes, you try."

Liz needed no more encouragement. The Don sat by benignly while Adelina helped Liz into the dress, tying tapes, doing up hooks and eyes, fluffing out lace. Once the dress was on, she then made up Liz's face as though for a performance, before fitting a wig of shiny black hair, which she carefully arranged over Liz's own hair after pinning it flat to the head so that it could be hidden under a small, elasticised cap. The last to be added was the jewellery; necklace, earrings and matching bracelets of pearls and diamonds – paste, of course – and the fan, a delicate affair of ivory lace. Pursing her lips, she circled Liz, twitching the skirt here, arranging the neckline there, smoothing down a stray hair, siting the necklace

86

just so, so that it shone against Liz's creamy skin. With a satisfied nod she then turned Liz to face the mirrors which lined the doors before directing a stream of rapid Italian at the Don, who nodded smilingly.

Liz's jaw dropped. That beautiful, dazzling creature was not her! Full bosom bared, forearms round and smooth under their fall of lace, face glowing under the high-piled hair. She had caught only one word she understood of Adelina's Italian: the word *bellisima*. It was enough. And as she looked at herself, she saw it was true. She bit hard on her lip. Never in her life had she thought to look like this.

"You see," the Don said to her indulgently, "all you needed was polishing then adorning."

"I don't recognise myself! This costume makes me over."

"No. You merely realise your assets."

"To know that I possess them is itself a miracle. Thank you, oh, thank you so very, very much!" Throwing her normal restraint to the winds with her hang-ups she threw her arms around him.

She spent the rest of her week at the villa, sleeping at the inn, spending her days in the company of a man who urged her on as she excavated her newly discovered self. Every day she tried on a different dress and wig, unable to get enough of the beautiful stranger who looked back at her from every mirror. She used the Don's approbation as the cement securing the newly laid foundation stone of her confidence.

On her last night, they all dressed up; the Don in his greatest role, Liz as Donna Anna, Adelina as Donna Elvira. They had a gala dinner – prepared earlier by Adelina so that all that had to be done was put the prepared dishes in the oven, and afterwards, Adelina sang to them. The Don had been right; her voice was creamy, her *legato* effortless, her resonance thrilling. The Don demurred, when asked if he would sing, saying he would rather smoke a cheroot, so Adelina went in to check on the coffee.

"I think," Liz said, high on success and wine, "that I have stepped out of real life and into a dream."

"We all have them, but I am happy to have been instrumental in helping you to realise yours. I only wish I could see you, but Adelina has described you perfectly, so I feel that I can. She has that gift."

"She is – remarkable," Liz said delicately. There were things about the relationship between the Don and his mistress/house-keeper she still did not quite understand, such as why a former mistress had become a housekeeper who acted towards him with none of the familiarity of the former but all the respect of the latter, but it was none of her business. The Don, however, was acutely perceptive.

"You are curious about Adelina, are you not?"

"I find her fascinating," Liz replied truth-fully.

"She is. Years ago we were very much in love. Now, we love each other. There is a difference, one of which you, as yet, know nothing. But you will know it, I hope, in time."

Liz said nothing.

"When one is young, love is more pain than pleasure. Inexperience and uncer-tainty lead to ineptitude and mistakes that can maim and destroy emotionally. The young demand certainty, about the one thing of which one can never be certain, and where the emotions are concerned, fear is a serial killer. To love and be loved is one of the greatest experiences in life – perhaps the greatest. I myself have been lucky enough to experience it several times. I hope you too will experience it, but if you are to do so you must not let the prejudicial opinions of others dictate the course of your actions. Always remember that you are the architect of your own life. It is what *you* think, what *you* believe, that matters."

Liz still said nothing. She did not even know if what she felt for Tom Carey was love or infatuation, she only knew she felt it, that he deeply affected her physically and emotionally, as no other man had ever done before, and that she wanted more, much more of him than she had.

"This man," the Don asked, interrupting her silence, "he is important to you?"

"Inasmuch as I know I would very much like to be important to him."

"Well then, we must hope that now you have discovered your true self he will be as captivated by it as you are. One must love oneself before one can love another, and this week you have begun to do so. I hope that you will – once others discover the true you – not forget the man who was there at its unveiling."

"Oh no, never!" Liz protested passionately. "I owe you more than you will ever know!"

"I too, have enjoyed your company. You

have amused and entertained and indulged me in my fancies. You know by now how much I appreciate beauty. You have much – are much. I envy the man who will claim it one day. My own interest in you is as a god-father."

"Fairy godfather more like!"

The twinkle she had come to know was in his voice. "Ah … but these … trappings have served only to give you an insight into your possibilities and a great deal is now possible, believe me."

"Do you believe in fate?" Liz asked after a moment.

"But of course! I am half Italian."

"I think it was fate which guided me here; made me stop at that particular inn, took me for that walk, made me pass through an open gate … I was in a very dark tunnel and there was no light anywhere; now I can see not only light but a whole new world. I am still not one hundred per cent sure of myself, but thanks to you I reckon I am at least seventy per cent. Thank you so very much for making this week a turning point in my life. Cinderella must leave this ball now that midnight has struck, but there will, I am sure, be lots of balls from now on."

# Five

On the following Monday morning Liz had not been in her office an hour before her phone rang. Mrs Stevens, Tom Carey's motherly secretary, wanted to know if she could spare Mr Carey five minutes before he left for Paris.

Oh, God! was her instant, clenched-stomach reaction. Was he still angry with her and her stupid snide comment? It had been quite uncalled for; the memory made her wince. But her knowledge of him – every nugget carefully filed and classified – informed her that he was not a man who sulked or cherished grudges. Still, there was only one way to find out and that was by facing him. If necessary, she would apologise.

But when she went into his office he was standing in front of the wall where the story-board for the new aperitif account was displayed.

"I thought you might like to know that the client is thrilled with your ideas," he told her. "The campaign goes ahead as per your story-boards." His manner was his usual one and there was no chill in the air.

"Good," Liz said, relieved on both counts.

His blue-green eyes appraised her before he asked, "How was paradise?"

The amusement in his voice and the teasing quality to his smile enabled Liz to reply truthfully, "It surpassed all my expectations."

"It shows." Something – or somebody? – had turned her on. There was a positive glow emanating from her. The sixty-watt bulb had been replaced by a halogen lamp. "You should go to paradise more often if this is the result," he observed.

Meeting his eyes Liz thought, *You don't know the half of it*, hoping passionately that one day, if fate would grant her another miracle, he would be going there with her.

Her first step in the remaking of Liz Everett was to take up Jilly's offer. She came to Liz's flat with her bottles, brushes, sticks and powders, and they spent an evening experimenting. Jilly reshaped Liz's eyebrows before re-contouring her face with blushers, gleamers and shadows, carefully defining its strong but elegant bones, the delicate hollows beneath the cheekbones, the classic line of her jaw. She emphasised – with three different colours – the muddy green eyes, turning them to jade. She outlined the full lips with one colour before filling them in with another and glossing the whole so that they gleamed like temptation itself. Liz was astounded at the number of aids used to make up her face so as to look as unmade-up as possible, but the result was mind-boggling.

"This is me?" she asked disbelievingly. "I never looked remotely like this when I wore make-up before."

"I told you. There is an art to making up a face and you probably did not possess it. Most women don't. They think all you need is a bit of powder, some blue eyeshadow and a pink lipstick."

My Aunt Louise for one, Liz remembered.

"Wrong! You need much more than that, and you have to use everything the right way. Now that we know what your face needs, the next thing we have to deal with is your hair."

She took Liz to her own hairdresser. "A well-kept secret among the *cognoscenti* so don't breathe a word. He is a magician but you don't have to take out a mortgage to pay his bill. You would do well to listen to his advice. I've never known him go wrong yet."

His advice was not to have her hair cut but thickened with his special shampoo then streaked with blonde highlights. "It is too fine and not thick enough to hold a short style without either a perm or lots of laquer and that never did anybody's hair any good. I see it streaked blonde and given body but worn the way you already wear it except with a bit of height in front to balance the length of your face, and a little less severity at the temples. That way it also exhibits the line of your throat, see ..."

After the face and hair came the body. "From now on you will wear clothes that do you favours," was Jilly's order. She took Liz to a shop in South Molton Street.

"I can't wear that!" Liz looked askance, when the assistant brought out a short black dress.

Jilly was having none of it. "Of course you can. Look at the way it is cut. It skims the figure, rather than hugs it. And with those blonde highlights and your creamy skin, black is your colour. So is this ..."

"This" was a trouser suit of silk velvet the colour of a ripe aubergine, with which Jilly picked out a see-through shirt of crisp organza the subtle pink of a new opened magnolia. "Which calls for an eye-riveting bra …"

Liz had never worn such exquisite lingerie in her life. Sturdy had been her watchword, but the lady at Rigby and Peller measured her to the last centimetre and provided wisps of silk and lace which not only supported but displayed. Liz clenched her jaw when she learned the price but bought three. She also bought the panties to match.

Jilly exhorted her to buy the sort of clothes she had always eyed and sighed as "not being for me". Now, since Jilly assured her they were, she splurged on a low-cut, long-sleeved dinner dress of raspberry pink crepe which clung like a second skin, outlining the swell of breast and hip. For the very first time, when it was being fitted, Liz saw envy in another woman's eyes, after which she left her qualms in the bin with the price-tags. Until Jilly said, "Now we have to test this on a suitable market. Roger and I have an invitation to a housewarming next Saturday. It's open house. The perfect opportunity to try out the New You."

Liz immediately panicked. It was one thing to make up and dress up in the security of flat or shop, it was another to chance her arm – not to mention her luck – in a houseful of strangers, especially the men.

"Now look," Jilly warned, "it is of no earthly use you taking all this trouble – not to mention spending all this money – for nothing. You are coming with us if I have to drag you kicking and screaming all the way to Highgate! Yours is no longer a light to shine unseen. Besides, who knows what its light may reveal ..."

It revealed Geoffrey, a lawyer who took one look at Liz in her velvet trouser suit and asked to be introduced. He was charming, pleasant, obviously attracted, so she used his admiration to nourish her burgeoning self-confidence. For the first time ever she had a social life, and when her phone rang it was not a wrong number, because she had also met a graphic artist whose work was mainly designing CD covers and posters for a major record company. At the other end of the spectrum from the ultra-conventional Geoffrey, his name was Marcus Steinberg and he had moved in on Liz the moment he set eyes on her in the "little black dress" at the party given by

Jilly's lover, Roger, to celebrate his winning an architectural award. She was, he told her admiringly "right out of a Renoir" and he would love to paint her himself, some time.

Whereas with Geoffrey Liz went to first nights, concerts, exhibitions and dinner in elegant restaurants, Marc – he did not like the name Marcus – took her to smoky pubs and jazz clubs where groups sat round large tables and, when they were not listening, argued, mostly about Art. He also tried to take her to bed the very first night but Liz told him firmly she did not go in for casual sex – or any kind of sex until the man was right, she added privately, and she knew at once that Marc was not. Instead of dropping her, as she expected, he shrugged, said "Okay, but you can't blame a guy for trying," before asking if she would like to go to a retrospective at the Tate.

Back at the office no one knew anything. There, she was still the old Liz Everett. As yet she did not have the confidence to try out the new one on Tom Carey. He was too important to fail with, besides which, he was tighter than ever with Melanie, and the young green shoots of Liz's self confidence were not up to withstanding the blight of that kind of competition. So during the day she continued to be the common moth. The butterfly flew only at night.

After several months of nocturnal flights Liz had found her wings as a woman, and that woman had her lawyer friend very much in thrall. He took her out more often than Marc – who was involved with a whole coterie of women among whom he generously distributed his favours – and their relationship was developing nicely. Unlike his opposite number, he had not rushed her sexually – he was both a cautious and circumspect man, a worshipper rather than a womaniser – which was why she continued to see him. Marc she did not take seriously; he made no bones about what he wanted, and was confident that it was only a matter of time before he got it. His ego's rationale was that Liz was playing hard to get. It would never have occurred to him that he just did not appeal to her that way, that she never for a moment took him seriously once she knew just how unserious he was about everything except Art. But he was fun, and he took her to places that were new and different. Most important of all, he played a key part in her crash course in The Games Men and Women Play.

Lingering over coffee after their third dinner together in ten days, Geoffrey said: "I have tickets for the new Pinter tomorrow. Will you come?"

"I should love to, but are you sure you are not a sucker for punishment?" Liz teased, in reality deeply pleased. That he kept on wanting to see her she took as proof that it was not just the pretty wrapping he liked: the woman it contained was equally important.

"You are no punishment. You are a delight. I can't seem to spend enough time with you. I love our time together. In fact," he reached across to take her hand, "I love you."

The only thing Liz found surprising was her lack of surprise. Here she was, being told by a personable, eminently catchable man that he loved her, and she was receiving it as calmly as the weather forecast. You should be doing handsprings, she admonished herself. A few short months ago you were despairingly surveying the world from the highest of shelves; now here you are being offered two loving arms to help you down and the only response you can think of is: "Thank you, but no, thank you."

"To be honest," Geoffrey went on diffidently, "I thought you would have guessed by now. Not being a particularly demonstrative man, I have probably not made it plain enough to you."

"No," Liz said on a smile he did not recognise. "That was me ..." At his puzzled stare she squeezed his hand. "Yes, I had noticed."

"But not in the way I notice you. You don't, do you? Share my feelings, I mean."

"I like you a lot. I like going out with you."

"But only that? You don't see me as more than a pleasant companion?"

"Not yet." Not ever, Liz thought, on a guilty pang, for Geoffrey was a nice man, a good man, but another man had got there before him and dug himself in, so deeply she would lose part of herself if he were to be removed.

"But you will let me go on seeing you? At least that way I can work on presenting my case."

"I have every intention of letting you present your case," Liz encouraged him, with a smile that caused the woman advancing down the restaurant with her companion and nearing their table to stop dead in her tracks.

"I don't believe it!" she gasped, in a voice

101

that said it had better not be true. "That's never Liz Everett over there."

The man with Liz laughed at something she said.

"Oh, yes it is," Tom Carey confirmed.

"But what on earth has she done to herself?" Melanie's voice threatened retribution to whoever was responsible.

"Isn't it obvious?"

At the note in his voice Melanie scowled. "Well, I intend to find out why." She had darted away before he could stop her. "Well, well, surprise, surprise ..." she shrilled, stopping at the banquette where Liz and Geoffrey were sitting. "Liz Everett, of all people – I actually didn't recognise you. What *have* you done to yourself?" And why? remained unspoken, hovering in the air threateningly, as Melanie's radar registered the raspberry red dinner dress and the creamy cleavage it showed, the exquisitely made-up face, the gleaming twist of hair dressed so as to show off the blonde streaks to best advantage. "I mean ... such a transformation! Whatever happened to the sackcloth?"

"I threw it out with the ashes," Liz told her serenely, head high even as her heart kicked in like a compressor. Looking straight at Tom Carey, she found he was looking at her so she acknowledged him graciously. "Tom."

She could have sworn his mouth twitched but he was equally gracious. "Liz."

Geoffrey had risen to his feet and Liz was about to introduce him when Melanie got there first. "Hello," she purred. "I'm Melanie Howard. Liz and I are old friends ..."

Geoffrey glanced at Liz uneasily, aware of the swell of bitchery, yet 'friends' had been said. Liz made the necessary introductions.

"I said to Tom, *that* can't be our Liz; not our own, penny-plain Liz Everett," shrilled Melanie venomously.

"Only during the day. At night I am tuppence coloured," Liz allowed, finding she was enjoying this.

"And worth every penny," Tom agreed smoothly, unleashing a smile Liz felt down to her toenails, before taking a grip on Melanie's elbow that had her glaring at him furiously before he bore her unwillingly away.

"What on earth was that all about?" Geoffrey asked, obviously baffled.

"Office politics. Melanie Howard and I are not now, never have been and never will be friends. That is a fiction it suits her to maintain. We once shared a flat for a short time, and right now she happens to be the Face in a current make-up and perfume campaign my agency is handling. Tom Carey is its Creative Director."

"Oh, I see." Then, "What did she mean, that she did not recognise you?"

"Do you think I go into the office all dolled up like this?" Liz made it sound droll.

His face cleared but his eyes went over her meaningfully. "I rather hoped you dressed that way for me."

"And if I didn't dress or look like I do, would it matter?"

"Well, it was the way you look which first caught my eye, but it is you, the woman, who has me hooked."

"But it was the cover which made you want to read the book?"

"I suppose so. Why? Does it really matter? What matters is that I am totally absorbed in it."

"Then that *is* all that matters," Liz told him warmly.

They left the restaurant ten minutes later and she did not turn to see who it was who watched her go. But somebody did. She could tell by the tingle between her shoulders. Probably where Melanie had sunk her knife.

— The following morning, since the cat was well and truly out of the bag she threw the latter away and put on one of her new, well-cut trouser suits, this one in pistachio green linen. She did her face as Jilly had showed her, let a few fronds of newly streaked hair cluster about her face and nape, then sailed into battle.

A couple of weeks later, Liz was in her office at the end of the working day, chatting with Bertie Fry, Ben Webster and a couple of fellow copy-writers from their group who had made it a habit – since her metamorphosis – to drop in at around six for a drink and a gossip. Ben – like all of them – was a much married man, with a quiverful of children, but he had made it obvious to Liz that she only had to say the word and he would not catch the 6.44 to Purley. Which word Liz had no intention of saying. Two more faces appeared round the door. Alec Sawyer and Ray Wallis, also members of Liz's group.

"Room for two more?" Alec asked, brandishing a bottle.

"After you two it will be standing room

only," Liz warned. "Don't you all have homes to go to?"

"Yes, but they don't have you as part of the furnishings," Ray sighed.

"My dear Ray, I have been part of the furniture around here for a long time now and nobody so much as gave me a second glance."

"Ah, but that was before you had yourself re-upholstered."

In the midst of the general laughter her office door opened again and this time Tom Carey stood there. Liz's laugh died. It was the first time he had let it be known that he was so much as aware of the nightly get-togethers.

"This *is* the Liz Everett fan club?"

"Want to join?" Bertie enquired. "I'm its Secretary."

"And we are all Life Members," Ben added.

"The subscription is a bottle," Alec offered. "Whisky, gin ..."

"Would vodka do?" Tom produced a bottle of Smirnoff. "My formal application for membership," he said, proffering it to Liz, who managed to say, "Granted. Will you have a drink to confirm your member-ship?"

106

"That was the general idea."

Turning to the ice bucket Liz discovered it was empty. "The ice has all gone," she said, cursing herself for stating the obvious, but aware that even now, around Tom Carey she tended to come over all stupid, the more so lately because since the night when he had first seen her in all her refurbished glory, she had become aware of a tension between them.

"Not surprising, in this temperature," he said now, and she heard the laugh in his voice. "But I am all for my copy-writers getting together to discuss work-in-progress."

"Actually, we talk about anything but work," Bertie confided.

"I can imagine. However, as you are all present and correct—"

"Speak for yourself," Alec quipped saucily.

"I might as well tell you that the *Le-Beau* Watch people want to meet us tomorrow instead of Friday." Turning to Liz, he asked, "Is your presentation ready?"

"Yes ..." She indicated her story-board along the far wall, and he went over to study it. When he turned back to her his eyes went over her charcoal grey, roll-necked cashmere sweater and matching trousers before murmuring: "Indeed ... your presentations have improved even on themselves ..."

—Liz gulped un-iced vodka and tonic. It was the very first time he had made verbal reference to her refurbishment, though she had been conscious of his eyes more than once, even if she found it difficult to meet them. Now, she was aware of that tension again, found it hard to look at him so glanced at her watch instead to find it was twenty-five minutes past six.

"Sorry," she said with relief. "I have to call Time, gentlemen, please."

"Got a date?" Ben asked enviously.

"As a matter of fact I have." Marc was taking her to an exhibition of what he called Street Art but she thought of as graffiti, in Whitechapel.

"Lucky man ..."

Acutely conscious of Tom Carey's steady gaze, Liz turned from it to bend down so as to pick up a glass which had been placed on the floor. As she did so, Alec, eyeing the trousers being pulled taut against her backside, sighed gently. Liz straightened with alacrity.

"Out!" she commanded. "Sigh no more, gentlemen ..."

They did as they were told. The new Liz may have changed outwardly, but she still spoke like the old one. There was a general chorus of "Goodnights" and "See you tomorrows" as her office emptied, but as Tom Carey made no move to leave, Liz busied herself tidying away.

Emptying his glass he came across, proffering it to her. As she took it, her fingers brushed his and she had to clamp down on the lightning bolt which zinged through her. Only with this man did physical contact produce an equally physical effect. Geoffrey's touch, like his kisses, was unstirring, ditto Marc. Yet this man, whom she did not really know, even though what she knew she liked more and more, could make her heart leap and her pulse flutter. Her sense of self-worth had grown considerably over the past incredible weeks, but he was the one man who had the power to scythe it off at the roots.

"Is your office the new Inner Sanctum?" he asked.

"I've always been known for my helping hand."

"I rather think they are more interested in helping themselves."

Tongue-tied for once, Liz was unable rise

to that. In no hurry to go, he wandered over to her drawing board, glanced idly at what lay there and then did a double-take, picking up the drawing she had been working on.

"What is this?" he asked.

Caught by something in his tone Liz went over. "I'm in the preliminary stages of a sketch which will, I hope, turn into a painting of a house belonging to a friend of mine." She had begun to draw the villa from memory, as she had first seen it, sugar-icing white in the moonlight.

"It's beautiful … Italy?"

"Would you believe Cornwall?"

"If you say so."

Caught by something in his voice and gaze Liz asked, "Why do you want to know?"

"It is exactly what I have been looking for. The house we had hoped to use for the Caribbean shoot in the *L'amoreuse* commercials is now no longer available; this one would be even better. It has everything and more. Would your – friend – permit us to use it for two segments of the commercial? Usual rates, of course, standard contract. The other four are in the can, but I was beginning to despair of being able to shoot

110

the finale in the setting I'd envisaged. This is exactly what I had in mind."

That was a fact. On the one hand Liz would like nothing better than to oblige Tom Carey. On the other, the thought of Melanie swanning around what Liz had come to think of as her own, private paradise was anything but pleasing. Nor did she know how the Don would react to being invaded by film crew and attendant paraphernalia. He guarded his privacy. That she had been allowed to become part of it was something she treasured. She had been invited to share it for two wonderful long-weekends since that first, paradisical week. After a moment, she said, "I don't know ... the owner is a very private person."

"It would not be for long. Three or four days, maybe five. It really is perfect for the purpose. I promise you we would not spoil anything and I would see that great care was taken to leave everything exactly as we found it." Tom paused then said: "I would not wish to spoil your paradise."

And she had thought the Don perceptive! Stunned, she met his eyes.

"It is where you went, isn't it?"

Unable to look away, she nodded.

"And this – friend – is special?"

111

Instinctively Liz smiled. "Oh, yes ..."

"Far be it from me to jeopardise a special friendship," Tom said, with emphasis on the *special*, "but if you could just ask him about the possibility I would be very grateful. And as quickly as you can, since if the answer is no I must keep on looking." He glanced down at her drawing again. "It is very romantic, isn't it?"

"Yes ... I can see Melanie too, floating down those terrace steps ..."

Tom flicked her an odd look from beneath lashes any woman would have died for, before saying politely, "I am keeping you from your date. Goodnight."

Now just how did he know the owner was a he? pondered Liz, when he had gone.

That night she rang Cornwall. It had become her habit to do so every weekend. The Don had suggested it after she had told him of her metamorphosis, being both deeply interested and encouraging of her efforts. Now, after explaining why she was calling in the middle of the week, she did as Tom had requested: asked him if he would be prepared to let the film company have the use of his house for approximately a week in order to shoot some segments of the story Liz had written: at a fee, of course, probably around a thousand pounds a day.

But what he asked was, "This Tom Carey … In your opinion, is he to be trusted with someone else's property?"

"Absolutely," Liz replied unhesitatingly.

"Then I suggest you bring him down to see me. I will talk to him, take his measure and then decide. Besides, it will give me an opportunity to see you again. Can you come down this weekend?"

"*I* can, but I shall have to ask him."

"Then by all means do so, and let me know the result."

"It is rather short notice," Liz warned. "He may have made other arrangements." Like another weekend way with Melanie.

"If he wants what he wants strongly enough, then he will come."

And he did. "I'd like nothing better," was Tom's immediate response.

"It is quite a drive so I would suggest we leave early Friday afternoon or Saturday morning."

"Friday. I want as long as possible down there to see if all is what I think it is. Who is he, your – friend?"

"His name is John diMarco."

Tom frowned. "Sounds familiar."

Liz did not enlighten him. Let him find out for himself.

That night she called Geoffrey to cancel their theatre date for the Saturday, and Marc to postpone their outing to an open air art exhibition at Greenwich on the Sunday afternoon, explaining that work called her away from London for the weekend. Both expressed disappointment. Both urged her to call them on her return.

She was ready and waiting – on tenterhooks – when Tom knocked on her office door at eleven o'clock. After trying on and discarding any number of outfits, she had decided it would give her game away to dress up to the nines, so she dressed down. Gap jeans and a cricket sweater in navy with white and green ribbing at the V-neck. She had made up her face to look as if it was innocent of anything but soap and water, and left her hair loose, tying it back with a bright scarf. She had washed it the night before, using another blonde rinse so that it gleamed gold where the light caught it.

Tom was as casual as she was in a pair of what she recognised as Nantucket reds faded to the rosy colour of ancient bricks,

114

and a matching shirt over a white tee shirt, bare feet in Timberlands. She recognised the style, having seen it on the men with whom she had waited once, to catch the plane from New Bedford to Nantucket, on one of her American trips. He's done this before, of course, she reminded herself. Just so long as he doesn't know you haven't.

"I'll have you know I am dying of curiosity," he said as they went down in the lift. "A Palladian villa in the wilds of Cornwall."

"Possess your soul in patience," Liz advised kindly. "All will be revealed."

"I am counting on it," he answered deliberately.

# Six

Tom's car was a navy-blue Saab Turbo 900SE convertible. Liz knew it well. She had seen Melanie getting in and out of it often enough. She wondered what he had told her – if anything – about this weekend, probably that it was because of her he was making the trek to the far west, the object being to place the jewel in its proper setting. The Don permitting, of course.

"So where do we head for?" he asked, as he put her bag in the boot.

"Well, do you want the fast route or the scenic route?"

"Have we time to take the scenic route? I mean, we are not in any hurry, are we? You said we aren't expected until this evening."

Liz could have sworn he sounded hopeful, but dismissed it as wishful thinking as she said, "Scenic it is, then. Take the M3 to junction 8; I'll direct you from there."

It was a bright, sunny day, though the

wind was chilly, but the big car was warm, added to which, Liz thought light-headedly, as the song says, I've got my love to keep me warm ...

"Now what are you smiling at?" he asked as he headed west, which made her realise he had been watching her.

"Anticipating the weekend," she fibbed, adding hastily, "and thinking that as we have a long way to go we should share the driving – if you don't mind letting me take the wheel of this very expensive piece of machinery."

"If you drive like you write I have no qualms."

No, but I have, she thought. This whole trip is something that hitherto only ever happened in my daydreams. That it was on business was secondary. That she was going with him at all was miracle enough to have her on edge, but her nerves quieted as they eased into comfortable conversation, exchanging information about each other's backgrounds. His father was a lawyer, a specialist in anti-trust law working for the State Department. His mother had been a political journalist, and, as they had both worked in Washington DC that was where he had been born. Unlike her, he was an only child. He had gone to University in the East – Dartmouth like his father, but although he had started out with the intention of becoming a lawyer he had soon realised he was not cut out to be one. He preferred advertising. He had started out with J. Walter Thompson in New York as a junior, and by the time he was twenty-four he was an account executive. He had spent the years '89 and '90 in their London office so he was no stranger to the city or the country, after which he had been head-hunted by BBD&O, where he had spent the next five years before being head-hunted once again by Hendricks-Mahon, whom he had left to come to BB&B. He liked the diversity of his job in spite of the pressure; the constant challenge, the satisfaction when a campaign succeeded and a satisfied client came back for more. In his opinion, advertising was an art form when done properly.

"But some of it is an insult to the intelligence!" protested Liz, who held strong views on the subject. "And, if I may say so, especially where you come from. I have watched commercials on American television that had me hiding my eyes! As for your penchant for 'knocking' copy ... It is a bad campaign when you are reduced to trashing your rivals."

"I agree, which is why I like working in England, where it is not allowed. However, it is the squeaky wheel which gets the oil, as an Englishman once told me, and you have to make people sit up and take notice – as you have been doing of late."

This had Liz instantly directing the topic away from a subject she was not yet up to discussing with him, of all people, and to a good-natured argument as to the relative merits of the different approaches to advertising in their respective countries. From there they progressed to music, where she was happy to discover that, like her, he had both a deep knowledge and love of it in all its varied forms, especially jazz. Like her he was an admirer and fan of Carmen MacRae and had not only heard of Pat Metheny but attended his last New York concert. He also agreed with her that Stephen Sondheim was the best thing to happen to the musical since George Gershwin, and had seen several of his that had never made it across the Atlantic.

"It seems we have similar tastes," he said, after they both solemnly agreed that there was nothing like a piano, a double bass, brushes on the drums and an artist like Ella, MacRae or Frank Sinatra making magic of a great standard. After which he put a cassette into his Blaupunkt which turned out to be Sondheim's *Company*.

Before Liz knew it, and because – another miracle – the traffic was not heavy, they had traversed the M3, by-passed Basingstoke and Andover, and were heading for Wincanton where, at Tom's suggestion, they stopped for a drink and a sandwich.

– He was effortlessly easy to talk to, and even when, now and again, they lapsed into silence, it was a comfortable one. The miles were absorbed into the conversation and when they arrived at Exeter, so skilfully had he driven even while giving what seemed like his full attention to her, that she felt obliged to suggest she drive for the last lap. He made no objection and as the afternoon was a lovely one, he put the top down. It was exhilarating to tilt her face to the sun's warmth, feel the wind flirt with her hair as well as the deep thrill of being with Tom and the anticipation of seeing the Don again, all to the driving beat of Pat Metheny's guitar.

Making excellent time, since their luck with traffic held, Liz drove across the top of

Dartmoor and down to Launceston, on down through Bodmin Moor to Truro and then the final lap down to Falmouth before taking the winding minor roads she remembered until she reached the Helford River.

She approached the house from the south rather than the north, since the Don had told her there was a road along the bottom of the valley which allowed cars to climb the gentler hill approach to the house and enter its grounds. Unconsciously she leaned forward. "Not far now ..."

Something in her voice had him asking: "What is it about this place?"

"You'll see." Liz promised mysteriously, and even as she did so it came into view, not white today but pink with the rosy fingers of the early evening sun. As he caught sight of it Tom leaned forward. "I see what you mean," he breathed.

"Told you," Liz said in a voice that had him turning his head to look at her, but she was smiling in the direction of Adelina, who must have been waiting, for she had appeared at the top of the terrace steps. All but falling out of the car, Liz took them two at a time.

"Adelina ... here we are."

Adelina smilingly took her outstretched hands. *"Benvenuto."*

"It is so good to be back."

Adelina's eyes went beyond Liz to where Tom was bringing up the two bags. Liz saw her eyes kindle with a look that was unmistakable. Yes, Liz thought proudly, isn't he though? Making the introductions she was surprised when Tom returned Adelina's welcome in Italian.

"You never said you spoke Italian."

"You never asked."

*"Il Signore* awaits you," Adelina prodded, proceeding to lead them through the house to the terrace at the back, where he was enthroned in his usual chair. Hearing them approach he stood up.

"Goddess? I would know that step anywhere." Taking the hands she held out to him he raised them both to his lips. "My nose also tells me where you are ... I am glad to see you are fulfilling your role."

At the twinkle in his voice Liz responded in kind. "I am not yet quite word perfect but I improve with every performance." Acutely conscious of Tom standing by she turned and said, "May I introduce Tom Carey. Tom, this is John diMarco, known to his admirers as 'The Don'."

The two men shook hands.

"Welcome, Mr Carey," the Don was affability itself. "I am so glad to meet you."

"One never refuses an invitation to Mount Olympus."

The Don clapped him on the shoulder. "I can see we shall deal together splendidly. I knew my goddess would not bring me anyone *antpatico*. Come, sit down, let me offer you both a refreshing drink after your long journey. Goddess, you shall do the honours while Mr Carey tells me why he wants my house."

Tom did so, briefly but concisely.

"Hmmm ... and it will be seen on television?"

"And in cinemas. I have two scenes in mind: one at sunset, which from the looks of that sky tonight should turn out to be spectacular, and one at night under the full moon due in ten days time."

"And this young woman, this 'face' around which you build everything, she is worthy of such a setting?"

"Perfect," Liz said, coming back with the drinks, "made for the colour camera. Black hair, white skin, sapphire eyes. In this setting she should sell perfume by the gallon."

"I can picture her," the Don mused, "but

tell me, why are you not the girl of this perfumed dream?"

"Because Melanie is already fixed in the
public's mind and eye as the face of the previous campaign," Liz explained. "Customer
identification is of vital importance in
advertising."

"But you do have a part in it all?"

"Liz wrote the running story," Tom
answered for her, "and the copy. She was
also responsible for the slogan which helped
make the first campaign so successful."

"And how did you come to know about
my house?"

"I happened to see a sketch she was doing
of it and asked her where it was. The rest
you know."

Turning to Liz, the Don said, "And this
sketch – where is it?"

"In my office."

"Then when you finish it I hope you will
let me have it. Better still, why don't you
paint the finished picture while Mr Carey is
busy with his commercial. That shall be my
only fee."

"Oh, but I'm never involved in the actual
making of the commercials. My work is
done long before the campaign gets to that
stage."

"As a favour to me. You know how much I appreciate your company."

"Well, I—" Liz looked at Tom uncomfortably. It was smoothly done but it was still blackmail.

"A painting by Liz – who paints very well – is a small price to pay," Tom agreed.

"Nevertheless it is my fee."

It was lightly said but the words "take it or leave it" hovered like smoke.

Tom turned to Liz. "Is such a fee all right with you?" His eyes bored into hers.

"If it is all right with you," she countered.

"Then so be it."

"One thing more, how long will you need to be here?" asked the Don.

"Well, a lot depends on weather conditions, but if they continue as they are – and the forecast says they will – I should say a day or so to set things up, another two to do the actual shooting, another day to clear everything away. I think five days would be a fair estimate."

"Good. Then Goddess here, shall be my eyes and ears – my agent, in fact. You shall liase – if that is the word – with her. Is that all right with you?"

"I have no complaints," Tom answered.

But Liz was dismayed. What on earth was

125

the Don playing at? The one thing she was *not* going to do was play pig in the middle where Melanie was concerned. She had thought to do no more than introduce the two men, see the proposed venture off the ground then wait and see the results. This would be her first time seeing the actual filming of her work. But Tom was a key player on this one, no doubt on the instructions of Francois Jourdain, who was a "hands-on" client. Now here was the Don putting her centre stage as his "agent". He was a persuasive – and manipulative she now realised warily – man, but Tom was no pushover. Truth to tell, she was sensing a slight … not atmosphere exactly, more a quivering of the air between them, as though from the bristling of fur. She also had the uneasy feeling that the Don was needling Tom. Why? Didn't he like him? What was not to like about Tom Carey?

"Well, Goddess?" chided the Don, waiting for her answer.

"I was thinking how I was going to manage to do both jobs: paint your picture and liase with Tom."

"Ah … but surely, a young woman of your capabilities can do both?"

Liz burst out laughing. "Do you always

get what you want?"

"If I want it badly enough."

Liz found herself flushing slightly, conscious of Tom's eyes.

Considering the matter settled the Don went on to announce blithely, "As we are having Mediterranean weather we shall eat out of doors tonight." Feeling for his braille watch, he added, "and I think it is time you were shown to your rooms. You are in the Botticelli room, Goddess. Mr Carey is in the Raphael room. I call my rooms after the paintings hung in them," he explained to Tom blandly. "A little conceit of mine. Goddess, you know the way."

As they mounted the carved and painted staircase, Tom said, "Now I see why you are an opera buff. But he hasn't sung in public for years. How come you know him?"

"A long story," Liz evaded, not up to recounting that True Confession to anyone, much less Tom Carey.

"I am a good listener."

"It will keep for now."

"Ah, but will I ... ?"

Startled, she turned her head to meet a gaze that had her looking away quickly. "This is your room," she said hastily, opening its door. It was dominated by a large painting of Lorenzo the Magnificent.

"Don't tell me: your Botticelli is Venus. Is that why he calls you Goddess?"

Liz shrugged, made a *moué*.

"Part of your long story?" There was something like derision in the dark brown voice. "I hope you will tell me some day."

"When I know you better," Liz fended lightly.

"That can be arranged."

Liz opened and shut her mouth like a fish. He was flirting with her!

"Which is your room?" he went on.

It was all Liz could do to say, "That one," nodding at the door across the corridor.

"And what time is dinner?"

"Eight."

"I'll give you a knock at seven-thirty, all right?"

"Fine," Liz agreed faintly.

He went into his room and shut the door.

She had brought her newest dress with her, as much to show the Don how far she had come as much as anything, but once she had showered, done her face and hair and put it on, when she looked at her reflection in the big mirror her nerve failed her. It was very pretty, very feminine, of layered chiffon in various shades of caramel, from milky to burnt-sugar, with a draped bodice held up by shoestring straps, and what was known as a handkerchief skirt of calf length, but it was low cut. When she had bought it, the reaction of the sales staff had been positive, to say the least. Now, facing her reflection and looking at herself as Tom Carey would see her she did not mind that the straps bared her shoulders; her qualms stemmed from the way the bodice showed her deep cleavage. She tried to tug it higher but it would not come. It was not that it was salacious, exactly, it just left her feeling ... overexposed. The last thing she wanted was for Tom Carey to think she was doing a Demi Moore, even if what she had was all her own. She was preparing to change it, deciding she was not yet ready for such a dress, when someone knocked at her door. Checking her clock she saw to her horror it was exactly seven twenty-five. Tom! Oh, God ... she had wasted too much time in front of the mirror ...

"Coming," she called wildly, making for the wardrobe, when the door opened and he came in. He must have thought she called, "Come in."

Totally overthrown she whirled to face

him, the chiffon floating about her long legs, feet in strappy gold sandals. He stopped dead in his tracks, his easy smile fading as for five seconds they stared at each other, then he was his usual unflappable self again as he said, "Good heavens, a punctual woman. I never thought to see the day."

*And that's not all you are seeing,* Liz thought. No wonder he looked dumbfounded. I *do* look like a tart. *Oh, God, I wish I had never brought the damned thing ...* But it was too late now. The deed was done.

He was wearing what she recognised as an Armani suit in dark grey; very understated but very elegant. As he stood back courteously to allow her to proceed him it was all she could do to keep from breaking into a trot. She could feel his eyes on her, was sure that her over-exposure was also blushing.

The Don awaited them on the south-facing terrace, where the table had been laid with heavy lace place-mats, ornate eighteenth-century silver and engraved crystal glasses. Tall white candles burned in protective storm lanterns, while the centre-piece of freshly picked white roses perfumed the air. The moon was a thin crescent. By the time of the shoot it would

130

be full and heavy.

"Oh, how lovely!" Liz exclaimed.

"As I am sure you are," the Don said gallantly. "Am I not right?" he turned to Tom.

"Aren't you always?" Tom returned evenly.

"Tell me what you are wearing," the Don commanded Liz.

"A caramel chiffon dress."

The Don turned to Tom, "Goddess tends to understatement. Describe it to me, if you please."

"Soft, floating and one hundred per cent female."

The Don smiled. "That is more like it. Come," he commanded Liz, patting the chair next to his. "Sit by me. We are having champagne so that we may drink to the success of your – how do you term it – shoot?"

Adelina appeared with the champagne in its cooler. She was in velvet, a dramatic dress the colour of blood, which also bared her sumptuous shoulders, and there were long strands of what looked like rubies in her ears.

"Tonight, we are *en fete*," announced the Don expansively, which was why he was no doubt wearing a suit that had hints of Spain about it, from its short jacket to the shirt frills at front and cuffs. Don Giovanni for the 1990s? wondered Liz, only to hear Tom murmur softly, "A 20th Century fox?" She shot him a startled look. "Think about it," he advised.

"It is not often I get the chance to enjoy such an evening," the Don continued, "and at my age one must make use of every opportunity. Perhaps you would do the honours, Mr Carey?"

"My name is Tom."

"Tom, then, please, if you would be so kind as to pour the champagne."

When they all had a glass, the Don raised his: "To *L'amoreuse*." He drank deeply, before musing, "A clever title, but then, you are selling love, are you not? In the guise of a perfume, of course." The voice was inoffensive, creamily bland even, but the needle was definitely out again.

"No," Tom corrected, his own blandness more than equal to the task. "Love that can be bought is not love. What we are selling here are dreams."

"Ah … we all have them, of course. Even you?"

"Why should I be different?"

I'm putting a stop to this before it goes any further, Liz resolved grimly before intervening to ask, "What culinary surprises have you in store for us tonight?"

"Wait and see," the Don answered mysteriously. "But it will not be ambrosia, even if this is Olympus. Nor am I Zeus, though we do have our Juno, do we not?"

It's me! realised Liz with a force ten seismic shock. He is goading Tom about me! Somehow he has sussed out that Tom is The Man, and as he also knows that Tom does not know, the needle is obviously to prod him into some sort of awareness, hence his appointment of me as his "agent". Except that there is no way I am having Tom coerced into wanting me. She looked at the Don. I know you only want to help, she told him silently, but not this way. I have to do this on my own, make my own mistakes. Like this dress ... She resolved to ask the Don to allow her to do so at the first opportunity.

At the table he sat at the head, Adelina at the foot, Tom and Liz – and my damned cleavage, Liz despaired – facing each other across its centre. They dined first on wafer thin slices of *prosciutto* wrapped around fresh figs, followed by rack of lamb with garlic and rosemary, potatoes *lyonnaise* and tiny *flageolet*, finishing off with richly purple grapes, nectarines, pears and peaches from the Don's hothouse, along with a selection of cheeses, all washed down with wine from his Italian vineyard. As they left the table to take coffee Tom said appreciatively, "Well, you may not be Merlin but Adelina is certainly Morgana le Fay." Adelina, who, Liz had decided, understood far more English than she cared to admit, acknowledged the compliment with a complicitous smile. Liz went to sit in her accustomed garden swing. Dinner had been positively Lucullian, as well as a truce, the needle having been put away, but she was alert for it, and if she was reading Tom's response aright, so was he.

Coffee having been poured, when the Don said, "I think some music, don't you?" Liz agreed with alacrity.

"That would make the whole thing perfect," she said. And keep the conversation to a minimum. The Don got up and Adelina followed him into the house. "I take it back about him not being a wizard," Tom said into the silence. "He's a warlock."

"This whole place is magic."

"Well, he has certainly put a spell on you."

134

Her eyes flew straight to his, felt them pin her to her seat.

"Well ... he did sort of change my life ..." Even now she still lacked the confidence to tell him the story of that magical night, to reveal the truth of her repressed, self-loathing and how it came to be changed by a blind man's words.

"I hope you'll tell me how, one day."

"When I know you better," she evaded, devoutly hoping that one day she would. Already her *awareness* of him had grown into a need she was finding increasingly hard to handle.

"I already have that in mind."

*Only because the Don is flourishing me at you,* Liz thought bleakly. He undid her when he said things like that. All her buttons. She had learned to cope with predatory men to a certain extent; she would never be able to cope with him since her feelings for him had her tilted off balance all the time. Why, when it was what she wanted more than anything, could she not handle it? Handle him? She would give up the ghost if he was merely trying it on, goaded into it by the Don's needling. And yet ... Something had been sizzling, she belatedly acknowledged, since he had knocked on her door to take her down to dinner. Even Liz, inexperienced as she was, was woman enough to know when a man's attitude towards her changed. As Tom Carey's most definitely had. She flicked a glance at him, found he was watching her steadily. Watch it! she warned herself, her insecurity and years of neglect instinctively preparing for the worst. It is proximity, this dress and the Don's fine needlework. He has been making Tom aware of you since the minute you both arrived. This change in attitude is probably no more than customer response to your new packaging.

Just then, the Don and Adelina returned to the terrace, and behind them, from the house floated the first limpid notes of what Liz recognised as Debussy's *Beau Soir*, followed by the voice. It was Adelina's. Liz was familiar with that honeyed velvet, having gone and splurged on CDs not only of the Don, but of Adelina. Closing her eyes in anticipation she gave herself up to the music.

Adelina sang several songs after the Debussy, including Hugo Wolf's *Silent Love*, followed by Schumann's *Moon Night*, ending with what Liz thought of as one of the most heartachingly beautiful songs ever,

Faure's *Après un Rêve*. Deeply moved by the beauty of both music and voice she was nevertheless aware that each and every song had been about love. You crafty old devil, she thought despairingly. You must stop this, *you must!*

When the last note ended, she sighed and said, "That was unbelievably beautiful. Thank you, Adelina."

"Yes," Tom agreed quietly. "Thank you." Adelina flicked him a glance from under her lashes and smiled. Tom went on to ask, "Will you not sing for us, *Signore?*"

"Not tonight. Perhaps tomorrow ..."

More coffee was poured and they sat and chatted amicably, mostly the two men discussing America, which the Don knew well, having sung there many times over the years. Finally, he said easily, "It is late for an old man – no, do not disturb yourselves. For you two, the night is as young as you are. Finish the coffee, if you will. Breakfast will be at half past nine." He rose, went unhesitatingly to where Liz sat and bent to kiss her hand.

"Goodnight, my lovely Galatea. Goodnight, Tom."

Tom, who had risen to his feet, bid them both goodnight, stood until they had gone

137

inside the house then sat down again before observing sardonically, "That is an anything but *old* man. He cannot be more than fifty-something."

"Fifty-eight, actually."

"How long have you known him?"

"It seems like forever."

"He was something of a legend in his day."

"Now you can say you have met the Legend."

"You seem to be living it." When Liz did not reply, Tom continued, "Another of his little – conceits?"

"He is blind," Liz defended. "It amuses him."

"I am already aware of his marked sense of humour."

That damned needle, Liz thought. Too late to caution the Don. The damage had been done. Oh, well, she thought. No point in hanging around. "I think I'll go up," she said.

Tom did not move. "Where did you meet him? Italy?"

"No."

"All right, so don't tell me."

Liz longed to, but his curt comment had the effect of eroding her confidence. To tell

Tom of the part the Don had played in changing her life meant confessing to so much else, revealing her inner self so totally that there was no way she could do it unless she was absolutely sure he would both understand and appreciate. He knew nothing of her emotionally crippled past, of the years of rejection and failure piled behind the newly furnished facade.

Into her silence, Tom said, "I take it then, that he is a closed book; a book of spells, naturally, since he is most definitely, from what I have seen and heard so far, a warlock. I am afraid I am only human." His voice was a saw serrated with frustration.

"So am I."

"Are you? I thought you were a goddess."

"That's just—"

"Another of his little conceits. Of which he has so many."

"How many have you?"

Surprisingly he laughed, and the edge was gone when he said, "That's more like it. All that sweetness and light is not you."

"You have no reason to complain, surely. You are getting what you want."

"How do you know what I want?"

"The use of the house."

"Ah, yes ... the house. Handed over for an

unbelievably small fee."

"Some people are never satisfied," Liz snapped, driven to it by the way the conversation was going.

"Some of us have higher expectations than most."

That was it! Liz jumped to her feet. "It's late."

"Only midnight. The witching hour. You are not about to change back into Cinderella, are you?" Liz winced. "But then, anything can happen in a fairy tale, at least, I hope so …"

The deepening note in his voice had Liz heading for the house, but he followed on her heels. "You know the house very well, I see. Well enough to see your way around in the dark. In fact, lately you give off a very bright light. Is he your alchemist?"

"You said you thought he was warlock. Make up your mind."

"I already have, but I still wish I knew a few of his incantations."

He was close behind her as they ascended the stairs, to find only one light burning in their corridor, but it was not dark since the half-moonlight streamed through the floor to ceiling window at the far end.

"Somehow I can't seem to find the magic

words where you are concerned."

They had reached her door, but before she could open it he had his hand on the ornate handle and kept it there, barring her way by putting the other one on the door itself so she was trapped between them. Liz seized up, staring blindly at her door. When he put a hand on her arm she quivered but was unable to protest as he turned her to face him, lashes lowered for protection for there was no way she could have looked him in the face. But she felt him bend his head, murmuring, "Let's see if actions do speak louder than words ..." before putting his mouth to hers. So wound up was she that her knees buckled and her hands came up to clutch him, unbidden and entirely instinctive.

His kiss was tentative and explorative at first, a light brush of his lips only, delicate as a butterfly wing-brush, then as her mouth opened to him it deepened and became something else as he gathered her to him in a tight embrace so that they were locked together down the length of their bodies, exchanging a kiss that seared the nerve endings. Liz had never been kissed like this before. Geoffrey's kisses had been reverent rather than passionate, while

Marc's had been greedy. This one was a whirlpool in which she felt herself being pulled under yet at the same time floating, out of her body, out of her mind, conscious only of his mouth, his tongue – *now* she understood what a tongue could do. His breathing changed, and as he drew her even tighter against his body, his hand coming up to cup the firm softness of her unconfined breast, she felt the hardness of him, which was when she panicked and tore her mouth from his, pushing herself away from him with her not inconsiderable strength.

"No!"

"Why not?" He made to recapture her.

"Because – because it is midnight and I am not sure what I might turn into!"

Before he could stop her she had twisted out of his embrace and was inside her room, slamming the door on him and leaning on it, trembling convulsively and gulping for breath.

When she could she reeled across to her bed to collapse face down on it, all jumbled inside, as though she had just come out of a spin dryer. She could feel her heart banging through the resilience of the mattress, was conscious of its beat at her fingertips but, most of all, at her lips. Being kissed by –

and kissing – Tom Carey was like falling off a mountain. Even thinking of it had her stomach dropping like a sky-diver. Only her inexperience had prevented her from losing all control because it had rung the bell for fright which had hammered on the door of her reason until she had no choice but to let it in. When at last she sat up her fingers were still trembling so that she could hardly undress herself. She did not do her usual face cleaning, she merely fell into bed like a drunk, re-living that kiss over and over again, emotionally and physically deeply disturbed.

When finally she fell asleep it was to dream about it.

# Seven

She slept heavily, and when she awoke and saw the time – 9.35am – leapt from her bed like a deer. The Don preferred punctuality but she was going to be late and that was all there was to it. She showered and dressed – navy Bermuda shorts and a sugar pink shirt – brushed her hair, tied it back, applied lipstick and mascara and then ran for it. But the Don heard her coming, even in rope-soled sandals, and rose to face her, as did Tom, who had to turn as he was sitting with his back to the house.

"Good morning! Sorry to be late. I over-slept." Her smile encompassed them both without meeting either pair of eyes.

"Good morning, Lazarus," Tom drawled, a laugh in his voice as he drew out her chair.

"Am I to take it that you are re-born, then?" chuckled the Don.

"Only after I've had breakfast," she retorted.

144

"Then eat! The coffee is fresh and the croissants are still warm."

Tom helpfully poured her a cup and placed the croissant basket within reach.

"Thank you," she said, still not up to facing him without blushing, and cursing herself for it.

"We have another beautiful day," the Don said. "What are your plans for it?"

"I'd like to go over the house and gardens, if that is all right with you," Tom requested. "Get an idea of the possibilities."

"Of course, of course! But that will not take more than the morning. After lunch, why not take my little boat on the river?"

"What kind of a boat?" asked Tom alertly.

"A sailing dinghy. I think that today the breeze will be just right. This morning the house, so that you may make your plans, Tom, and this afternoon you will go sailing and tonight – tonight we will have a gala dinner. How does that sound?"

"How about too good to be true?"

Today it was Tom's turn with the needle. There was a definite taunt to the dark brown drawl, but the Don only smiled complacently.

"Ah, but it is true, I assure you. You will find the boat moored at the jetty. Go down through the grotto and behind its rear door is a path which leads to a flight of steps; at their bottom you will find the boat. I have had it prepared for you. Once on the river there are lots of little coves where you may swim and sunbathe. I myself must work. I am writing my autobiography. I dictate it into a machine and my words are then typed up. I try to do at least one thousand words a day, more if the muse is flowing."

"Now *that* I have got to read," said Tom.

"I hope so. Now, if you will excuse me, I will make a start."

Liz, who had meant to have a quiet word with him, was again left high and dry. There was no doubt about it, he was a master strategist. Every last detail accounted for. Except one. Tom Carey was not going to see her in a swimsuit because she did not own such a thing, believing she was far too large to wear one. Swimming was out!

"Something on your mind?" asked Tom. It seemed he read faces as easily as the Don did voices.

"I've never sailed before," she answered, which was also true.

"Well I have, so you don't need to worry. You'll be quite safe with me."

The way he dropped his voice had Liz

turning to look at him. That teasing smile she had come to know was hovering around the mobile mouth and was reflected in his eyes. Of course, she thought sturdily. To him it was only a kiss, a harmless piece of flirting. He was used to it, accomplished at it. A thing like a kiss was of no possible consequence. God knows how many women he had kissed. How was he to know that for her it was a first?

Worry always sharpened her appetite so she demolished a couple of freshly baked croissants with butter and what her taste buds recognised as continental apricot jam, drank two cups of coffee and talked to Tom as normally as her hyper-awareness of him would allow.

After breakfast, she said, "I'll just go and get a notebook and pencil."

But Tom produced them both. "Always ready," he explained, and this time there was a definite gleam in the blue-green eyes. "I used to be a member of the Boy Scouts of America."

But he was all business when it came to examining angles and checking light. He had brought his Pentax and took a series of pictures, including one of Liz as she stood gazing pensively out at the gardens. "Just so that people will believe me when they see these photographs. Nobody will ever doubt *you* for a minute." He was flirting again!

"How come you know so much about camera angles and lighting and such?" she deflected.

"My college room-mate. He works in Hollywood. Right now he is a First Assistant Director, but he has hopes and ambitions to be the last name in the opening titles one day. He shot several of my commercials before going in to the movies and because of him I've been allowed on several sets. What I learned there comes in handy at times like these."

Then they went over the house, in case Tom wanted an interior shot. He whistled softly as he took in the paintings, the furniture, the porcelain and crystal. "No doubt about it, money *and* taste. He is a connoisseur, all right." This last oblique reference Liz knew was meant for her, but he did not take it further.

When they all met up for lunch – a superb *risotto al salto* – Tom was warm in his expression of thanks to his host. "This is even better than I had expected. Just perfect for our purpose, especially the fountain. Melanie's *L'amoreuse* face seen

through the spray will be a stunning shot …
I really am very grateful to you."

The Don waved that away. "Goddess
here, told me you were to be trusted, and I
trust her implicitly."

Tom turned to Liz. "Thank *you*," he said.

As they rose from the luncheon table
Adelina said to Liz, "I have something for
you," and produced a one-piece swimsuit in
her favourite dark red trimmed with a paler
pink.

Liz looked at the Don, but as he could not
see her he had no idea. But Adelina did and
advised him in rapid Italian because at his
most urbane he said to Liz, "I asked
Adelina to lend you one of her swimsuits
because you probably did not think to bring
one of your own … or did you?"

"No," answered Liz, the unspoken words
being *as you very well know*.

Turning to Tom, the Don said, "I can also
do the same for you, if needs be. I try to
anticipate my guests' needs."

"I've noticed," Tom told him. "And no. I
did not think to bring one either."

"Then Adelina will see to it for you."

Liz went up to her bedroom determined
to put a stop to the Don's little games. He
may have the best of intentions, she

thought, but Tom is probably thinking the worst so I cannot allow him to go on manipulating us in this way. The sooner I tell him to leave things alone the better.

When she tried on the swimsuit she found that although the front was cut high and straight across the collar bones, the back was deeply pared away, almost to the cleft of the buttocks. No way did this suit ever belong to Adelina, Liz thought askance. The label was Italian, from a fashion house in Milan, and it was obviously brand new, but it was not the kind of thing a woman of Adelina's age would wear. Truth to tell, it was not the kind Liz would wear either, but she had to admit that on her it did look good. There were no bulges, just a sleekly curved line of breast and hip, not to mention buttock. All the same, she decided, as she covered it with her shorts and shirt, it would be politic not to sit with her back to Tom at any time.

He was waiting for her on the terrace, carrying a large wicker basket, and they walked sedately through the gardens to the grotto, found the ornately studded iron door at the back, which gave onto the path which sloped down to the expected flight of stone steps and a small boathouse where the dinghy, painted a bright canary yellow, was tied.

Tom handed Liz in first, then gave her the basket before getting in himself, untying and hoisting the sail before loosening the painter, after which the light breeze took them out into the creek, which would eventually end at the river proper. The sun was hot, and Liz was glad of the breeze. She sat with eyes closed, her face tilted to the warmth.

"You are very quiet," Tom observed after a while.

"Nothing to say."

"That makes a change! What are you doing, mulling over the situation, waiting for the magic words 'take me'?"

Liz returned that ball with a backhand volley. "All bids to be submitted in plain paper envelopes to be opened at the same time."

"What's the competition like?"

"The best."

"No hints?"

"You bid blind or not at all!"

Too late she realised where she had fed herself and grimaced at her stupidity as Tom purred: "Ah ... of course."

She was about to blast him but he got in

first. "Head down, I'm coming about."

Liz ducked as the sail swung and the boat did an about turn. "Let's see what lies further up the creek rather than the river," he said. "I thought it looked rather inviting."

Depends on what kind of invitation you have in mind, Liz thought.

"What did he mean by a gala dinner tonight?" Tom asked, once he had the boat heading up-stream.

"No idea," Liz answered truthfully. "A surprise, perhaps. He is a man of surprises."

"So I have discovered."

His dry-unto-dust tone had Liz saying accusingly, "You don't like him, do you?"

"What makes you think that?"

"The way you speak to him; the things you say."

"That works both ways, or hadn't you noticed?"

Liz, who had, could not think of a way to explain why, so said nothing.

"On the subject of surprises, you have turned out to be no small surprise yourself."

Even now, some limpet-like residue of sensitivity as to her Amazonian status had Liz wincing inwardly at the word "small".

"How many more skins are there to be shed? Or was it just protective colouration, before? Too many predators?"

If only you knew, Liz thought, longing to tell him but, like the song said, afraid and shy.

"It's all part of the same story, isn't it? The one you won't tell me."

"There really isn't anything to tell."

"So you have renounced all your vows but that of silence?"

Seeing she was about to be caught between the proverbial rock and the hard place Liz opted for the nearest exit, which happened to be the water. "I think I'll swim," she said, and standing up she wrenched off her shirt and shucked off her shorts before diving over the side and swimming away strongly with her powerful crawl. When eventually she came up for air she turned, treading water, to see the boat some distance behind, its sail lowered, but no sign of Tom. Scanning the shore she still could not see him, until suddenly she felt hands seize her ankles and pull her under for a brief moment. She surfaced, spluttering to find Tom laughing at her. "So you are a mermaid too?"

She flung herself at him and for a while

they wrestled like two unruly adolescents, horsing around, splashing and playing tag until Liz challenged, "Race you to the boat," and was away with the powerful crawl her father and brothers – all championship swimmers – had taught her. But he was stronger and faster and caught her up swiftly, touching the side of the boat first.

"You swim very well," he complimented. "Nice style."

"You are no slouch yourself."

"I was in my College Swimming Team." With one lithely powerful movement he heaved himself up into the boat before reaching down a hand for her, pulling her up out of the water, hair and body streaming, the wet swimsuit plastered to her body. For a brief moment they stood breast to chest, thigh to thigh, then Liz moved quickly to sit down, careful to face him. Reaching for her towel she rubbed her hair, but from under it she was able to watch him covertly as he squeezed water from his own hair before using his towel to mop up the rivulets flowing down his broad shoulders and smoothly muscled chest. He was in excellent shape, and there was no sign of shortage of breath. His brief navy trunks likewise revealed no shortage of masculinity either. "What's the matter, have I grown a tail?" Too late she realised she had been staring and retreated under her towel. When she came out from under they were sailing upstream again and Tom was scanning the shore. "I thought we'd take advantage of this sun, do a little sunbathing to dry off, especially your several yards of hair ... I had no idea it was so long. You *are* a mermaid!"

"I have to be careful of too much sun," Liz evaded at once, determined not to lie around in this swimsuit and to dress again as soon as she was dry. "I burn easily."

"It's that fair skin of yours. Fortunately, your friend the Magus, who sees and knows all, provided us with not only towels but suntan lotion, sunglasses, and would you believe it, a vacuum chilled bottle of good wine? He leaves nothing to chance, does he?"

*No, the old devil most certainly does not,* Liz thought, exasperatedly, *but oh, how I wish he would ...*

"This is incredible weather for an English summer," Tom commented, as he headed the dinghy for a small, secretive looking cove which had a riot of wild, pale pink azalea bushes overhanging the water and what looked like a stretch of lush grass.

"When we get one we get a real one," Liz agreed.

"I for one will take reality over the virtual kind any day."

Was that a dig? Liz wondered uneasily. If so, at whom? Her, the Don, this blatantly manipulative weekend or the whole damned thing?

He tied the boat to a low-hanging branch, pulling it close inshore so that Liz could step out, before proceeding to unload the basket, firstly of two more big towels which he spread on the grass side before lowering himself on to one of them. Liz gingerly sat down on the other.

"There," he said. "That will do nicely, but before you get done to a turn I think I had better anoint you ..."

"We won't be here that long, surely ..."

"Says who? It is," he picked up his watch, "three o'clock. Dinner is at eight. We don't need to move from here until the sun does."

Rummaging in the basket he brought forth a large bottle of Ambre Solaire, Factor 15. Liz held out a hand but he said, "Back first, and as you can't reach I'll have to do it for you. Turn around."

Put up or shut up time, Liz thought, as

she did so. She felt him lift her damp hair out of the way. "Pure silk …" He raised several damp strands to his nose. "And do I detect perfume? I thought you did not buy dreams."

Jerking it out of his hands Liz tied it out of the way with her scarf.

"Right, on your front, please."

"I can just as easily stay in the shade."

"Why?"

There was no answer to that, so gritting her teeth she turned over, revealing the long line of her back and the enticing curve of her behind, revealed by the damply-clinging latex of her pared-away swimsuit.

Running a long trail of oil from her nape to just where the suit began, he began to spread it with long, firm strokes. Closing her eyes, Liz surrendered to the delicious sensations his hands were provoking, feeling her tension stretch itself hugely and then relax, boneless and replete.

"If you were a cat you'd be purring," Tom said, a laugh in his voice.

"Like Empress," Liz murmured.

"An Empress and a Goddess! That must cause problems with precedence."

Liz opened one eye. "Empress Rules, OK?"

He left her back to do her thighs and the backs of her legs, fingers firm and strong.

"You used to share with Melanie, didn't you?" he asked, lifting one foot to work oil into it.

"Mmmm …" So she had told him. And what else? Liz wondered.

"Lie still, I'm not finished yet. But you prefer independence?"

"It has become second nature to me."

"Choice or circumstance?"

"Custom and usage."

"So you are not entirely changing your image, then?"

"The ingredients are exactly the same and the mixture as before," Liz answered firmly.

"Except you have frosted the cake."

"We both work in advertising, we know what the right packaging can do."

"But when you have a first-class product the packaging is supernumary."

"And unless you market that product in a package attractive to the eye how are people to know?"

"Even the most desirable packaging will not, in the long run, continue to sell an inferior product."

"No, but it will help increase the sales of a superior one."

Tom's laugh was short. "I'll bet you play tennis as well as you swim. You always manage to return the ball."

"That's where I got *my* practice."

He had begun to apply cream to his own arms and chest. "Don't look now but your chip is showing."

"Which one would that be?"

"The one on your shoulder."

"That happens to be my head."

"That is no chip – unless it is the latest in Bill Gates' series of miracle workers. I am referring to the one your remodelling has not yet managed to whittle away."

Liz tried for a scornful laugh and thought she managed rather well. "What a vivid imagination you have."

"That swimsuit Adelina kindly 'loaned' you leaves precious little to it."

Liz at once sat up, drawing her legs protectively to her chest and wrapping her arms around them.

"If you put your wares on display you must expect them to be looked at," Tom pointed out reasonably. "You are the most amazing bundle of contradictions. One minute you are Ms Nobody from Nowhere, shrouded in what looks like standard issue, the next you are Lady Somebody from

Everywhere, but as soon as an appreciative comment is made you shoot from the hip! Surely you are aware that you and that swimsuit are a Queen-sized come-on!"

"It is not my swimsuit!"

"No, and it isn't Adelina's either. She is thirty years too old for it. That warlock up there is playing games and I don't see why I should join in when I'm not sure what his game is – although I have got a pretty shrewd idea."

Liz opened her mouth but again, there was nothing she could say without giving her own game away.

"No come-back? Does that mean I've won this round?"

Liz rallied her resources. "I would not class you as one of nature's losers."

"Then how would you class me?"

He had her backed into a corner.

"You are the best Creative Director I've ever had."

The quality of his smile told her she had blundered again, confirmed when he said silkily, "But you haven't had me yet." Liz gulped. Was that an invitation? "You know what I mean", she defended.

"That is precisely my trouble. What you say and do don't always match up – apart from your copy, of course, which always fits perfectly."

"I don't know you apart from work," Liz fended desperately.

"I repeat: that is easily remedied."

"But – why? I mean, I thought you and Melanie ..."

"Melanie holds no kind of monopoly on me."

"You could have fooled me." Again it was out before she could rein it in.

"Probably, but I have no intention of trying." Liz's mouth opened to protest at the slur but he over-rode her. "I am being honest with you about Melanie. I have certain – obligations – where she is concerned, and I fulfil them to the best of my ability. I have never attempted to hide that fact. Office gossip proves it."

So he knew what was being said! And did not care from the sound of it.

"You, on the other hand," he continued, "won't be honest with me. Like telling me what part that manipulative 'old man' in his sugar-icing house plays in your life. What magic did he perform on you? How did he manage to make the Common Brown Moth into the Scarlet Empress, because it was him, wasn't it? It is quite obvious that although he cannot see you he knows exactly where you are at."

"And what exactly does that mean?"

"It means that although he may have persuaded you that you are Sharon Stone, what you really are is Little Red Riding Hood, and make no mistake, under the father figure disguise is the biggest of bad wolves!"

Liz reared like a spurred horse. "That is absolutely not true! He has never so much as put a finger wrong where I am concerned! How dare you patronise me!"

"I would not pat you anything. You'd have my arm off at the shoulder before I knew what had bitten me. You wield a well-honed tongue but it is not nearly as hard boiled as you like to pretend. And do leave off stoking that fire of resentment; it is quite hot enough out here."

"You are the one burning Melanie at both ends!"

His smile had her gnashing her teeth. "How you do go on about Melanie. Do I detect a touch of the green-eyed monster?"

"Dr Frankenstein is not my GP." Getting to her feet with as much dignity as she could muster, she said, "I see no point in continuing this conversation. We may as well go back to the house since I seem to be ruining your pleasant afternoon."

"Did I say so?"

"You don't need to."

"So why put words in my mouth?"

"I know what I'd like to put in your mouth!"

"A gag? Your fist? Both feet, maybe?"

Liz could feel her cool melting rapidly in the heat of combustible emotions. Her instinct was to escape before she made him really lose his temper, because she could sense anger. "I'm not staying for this," she muttered to herself, but he heard her.

"Then stay for this." His hands shot out, seized her ankles and pulled her legs from under her so that she fell back onto the grass. In an instant he had her pinned, hands locked around her wrists, body over hers, kissing her with all the pent-up violence of a man frustrated beyond endurance. All it took was the touch and feel of him and Liz's rage was transmuted into pleasure. Her mouth opened and her eyes closed as he kissed her, almost punishing her with his kiss to start with until he became aware there was no need to pinion her and he slid his hands up her arms to her shoulders, where he pushed aside the straps of her swimsuit so that his hands could caress her breasts, her fondant pink nipples springing to attention as he did so. When he took one of them into his mouth Liz arched as a piercing sweetness shot through her. Again, he was the match that lit her feelings, which were reaching incandescence under the attentions of his mouth, hands and tongue, yet even so, in the midst of her own delirium she was aware that his own was raging out of control.

It was only when, through the fog of their intensity, they gradually became aware of clapping, whistles and cat-calls, that both realised at the same time they had an audience. As Tom lifted his head to look behind him, Liz raised her own to see a small motor boat chugging by, its passengers – all of them teenagers – hanging over the side, enjoying the view and applauding the action with encouraging – and lewd – gestures. Flushing a red so vivid it dimmed her by now round-her-waist swimsuit, Liz pushed Tom away violently with a strength increased by embarrassment and dragged it up to cover her naked breasts, adjusting the straps before rolling away from him, ending up on knuckles and haunches, regarding the scene in shamed horror from the tangled thicket of her hair.

Tom's face was as flushed as her own and his chest was heaving with his deep breaths, but he never took his eyes – their normally vivid blue now dark and slumberous – from hers as the motor boat slowly chugged its way past, leaving behind a silence that held its breath.

"It's all right," he soothed at last, as though gentling a spooked horse, "they've gone ..." He held out a hand, but when Liz recoiled, dropped it by his side. She had no idea she was regarding him with all the terror of a trapped rabbit. But she saw the way his face darkened. "It's practice makes perfect, not practice makes pervert," he threw over his shoulder contemptuously, as he bent to snatch up the towels, leaving Liz in no doubt as to either his anger or his conviction that she was, indeed, Little Red Riding Hood. How was he to know that she had ten years inexperience over the rest of the female population between the ages of twenty and thirty? Nor had he the slightest idea that she was top-heavy with feelings for him and scared she would overbalance, thus making him think she was a pushover, while always, hovering on the horizon like a pack of hyenas was her fear of rejection. It was no wonder he found it difficult to understand her contradictions. She did not understand them herself.

They dressed in frigid silence and sailed back the same way, Liz reading Tom's silence as that of one who, while he was of the opinion that least said was certainly best, did not give a damn about the soonest mended bit since as far as he was concerned the whole damned thing was beyond repair anyway.

Unable to get past her crippling insecurity, she sat with her back to him, holding her head high when everything in her wanted to turn on him and scream, "All right, I'll satisfy your curiosity!" But she lacked the courage, which only went to prove how right he was about her. Sharon Stone was indeed way beyond her capabilities. Little Red Riding Hood, on the other hand, she could play blindfold.

# Eight

At the jetty she left the boat without a word, striding off up the hill, leaping the steps to the grotto two at a time, slamming its door on him and the mess she had made of the afternoon before leaning back against it and allowing her rigid spine to crumple. Blowing her nose, she wiped her eyes hastily, for now was not the time to allow her feelings free rein. They would have to wait until she was in the safety of her room.

As she entered the gardens she saw that someone was sitting with the Don. A visitor – the very last thing she needed. What she needed was to hole up in her room in order to conduct a post-mortem on the death of her dreams. Instead, she would have to put on the performance of her life and hope that the Don, that most consummate of role-players, would not spot it was acting. He already knew too much: there was no way she was going to allow him to so much as suspect the fiasco she had just created.

Nearing the terrace, she saw that the visitor was a man and that he was young, personable; a blond Viking with a beard as yellow as his hair. He stood up as she reached them, revealing himself to be a veritable giant.

Alert as always to the very movement of the air the Don said, "Ah, is that you, Goddess? Come and meet another young friend of mine, Dieter Schuller. Dieter, this is Elizabeth Everett, my ... god-daughter." Liz held out a hand which vanished in the vastness of his as he bent over it.

"I prefer Goddess." His smile was dazzling and his English excellent, only faintly Teutonic.

"Dieter is a pupil of mine. He comes to me for a month each summer and I work him hard."

"A bass?" Liz hazarded.

"Of great quality. He will be a world-beater one day."

"That is why I come to you," Dieter said winningly.

"And where is Tom? I heard only the one footstep," the Don went on.

"Tying up the boat."

"You had a pleasant afternoon, I hope?

168

You were not gone long."

But Liz avoided that trap. Turning to Dieter, she said, "Are you the reason for our gala dinner tonight?"

"No questions!" The Don wagged a benevolent finger. "It is to be a surprise."

"I am already surprised to find such delightful company," Dieter said. Liz met a pair of frankly admiring baby-blue eyes and applied them as soothing balm to her badly wounded susceptibilities. Here was the means of defining and refining her just brutally exposed need for experience. By the time Tom arrived five minutes later, Dieter was sitting beside her on the terrace balustrade, as close to her as he could get without actually being thigh to thigh, flirting with the practice of an expert. Odd, thought Liz, as she fended and parried. There was no physical attraction whatsoever on her part although he was, she supposed, an attractive man. He was better looking than Tom in a Teutonic Knight sort of way, bigger than Tom, much more splendid of body, had undeniable presence and a great deal of best-butter charm, but he might as well have been a block of wood as far as she was concerned. Yet Tom had only to look at her and it was a case of heart thumping, skin pricking. Nor did Dieter's touch send an electrical charge zinging through her veins as Tom's did. Why was it she could handle the one so effortlessly yet constantly make an infantile fool of herself with the other? Was that what love did to you? Scrambled your brains?

She treated Tom, when he arrived, with the scrupulous politeness of a stranger who has no desire to take the acquaintance further. After all, there was now no point in trying. Which was when the Don informed them that dinner was to be a Special Occasion, asking that they please enter into the spirit of things. More than that he would not say. They would find out soon enough what he meant.

Liz did so as soon as she entered her bedroom. Laid out on her white bedspread was a black dress, demi-crinoline, in the style of the early Victorians; all Chantilly lace and silk ruffles, deeply *decollet*é. One of Adelina's, obviously. But which operatic heroine? Then she saw the violets embroidered onto the black silk of the accompanying fan. Violetta, of course!

For a moment Liz felt a hysterical desire to laugh. No one in their right mind was ever going to believe she was dying of consumption. Mourning, though ... oh, yes. The colour was spot on. Holding the dress up against her she saw it was exquisite, but she was in no mood for a gala dinner. Obviously the Don, knowing of Dieter's impending arrival and her own love of dressing up, had manipulated events yet again, intending no doubt to flourish her at Tom so as to make him see just how such masquerades enhanced her, since she became someone else when she was in costume. Nice try, she thought, but a waste of time. I am being consumed all right, but not by tuberculosis.

She shuddered at the way she had revealed herself. She could not have made her feelings for him plainer if she had set them to music and hired a band. He would have to be made of stone not to interpret her response to him for what it was. Except he was made of anything but stone. Let loose, Tom Carey was a tiger ... her stomach lurched at the memory, but it helped salvage some pride to know he had been every bit as carried away as she was; she had felt him grow against her thigh, hard enough to penetrate steel, at once terrifying and exciting to a virgin whose sexual experience was all in the imagination. Trouble was, his actions and physical response had been brought on by the fact that he believed she had come on to him by wearing that revealing swimsuit, even though she was not woman enough to carry it through.

She let go a long, hopeless sigh then stiffened as an idea hit her. Yes, she thought. Why not? What was to lose now? If that was what he thought, why not live up to it and at the same time play up to it? She was struggling to fasten hooks and eyes when Adelina knocked and came in, already sumptuously dressed in her favourite dark red, this time of heavy taffeta which rustled imperiously, and she had diamonds at throat, wrists and ears.

"You look fabulous!" Liz exclaimed spontaneously.

"*Grazie*, now I come to help you."

"Well, if you could do up these tapes and hooks and eyes. I can't quite reach ..."

When she took a final look in her mirror, Liz was pleased to see that she looked radiant. Her wig tonight was strawberry blonde, and suited her skin tone no end, while the black of the dress set off her creamy shoulders, its frills and flounces swaying enticingly as she moved. Adelina had taught her how to walk in such a dress, small running steps which made it seem she was floating access the floor. Now she added the finishing touches: a five-strand necklace of pearls and amethysts, with matching bracelets and earrings. Finally, Liz picked up her fan of silk, feathers and beads embroidered in the shape and colour of violets.

"*Che belleza!*" exclaimed Adelina. "You are Violetta! Now we go to show *Il Signore*."

He and Dieter were in the music room, both of them in the evening dress of the period, shirts befrilled and hands in white gloves. Dieter's eyes lit up at the sight of Liz. "Beautiful, beautiful," he crooned, kissing her hand with a click of his heels. "You take my breath away."

"The worst possible thing to happen to a singer." Liz tapped his arm with her fan as she had seen it done in period costume dramas.

"You approve of the dress?" asked the Don, in the voice of one who had no doubt whatsoever, having listened to Adelina's detailed description.

"It is fabulous, even though nobody in their right minds will believe me to be dying of consumption. However, I will do my best to live up to the rest of it."

"Then I am hopeful," Dieter hinted, in a voice heavy with meaning.

"Hope," she told him flirtatiously, "comes free ..."

He offered her his arm and they promenaded out into the hall just as Tom was coming down the stairs. He too was in the evening dress of the period and it suited him, the black setting off his tan and emphasising the dirty-blond hair. Liz took a deep steadying breath as his eyes went over her. Feeling her hand tense on his arm Dieter looked from one to the other watchfully. Then Liz made Tom a deep, mocking curtsey before sweeping past.

The table had been laid on the terrace again, and there were bottles of champagne waiting in silver coolers. The Don made the first toast, bowing in the direction of the two women, sitting side by side. "To beauty."

As the evening was so warm, dinner was cold. Antipasto, followed by fresh *saumon en gelée* with a rich mayonnaise, and a salad of radicchio, quails eggs, young asparagus and tiny new potatoes, finishing off with *pêches melba*, drinking champagne with every course.

Liz lost count of the amount she drank, since no matter how often she sipped from her glass it always seemed to be full. When they left the table she was floating in a way that had nothing to do with tiny steps, causing Adelina to murmur into the Don's ever receptive ear. It seemed to Liz that her blood had been transfused with wine, frothing and fizzling, blurring her vision so that everything and everyone seemed to have developed a halo. There was music, she realised. Where was that coming from? But when Dieter came up to solicit her to dance she got up with alacrity and let him waltz her into a state of almost total dizziness. As he led her back to her seat she accepted the cup of black coffee that was held out to her, only to realise, after she had emptied it, that it had been proffered by Tom.

"More of that and less Dom Perignon," he cautioned. "It's vintage and very potent."

"So am I," she told him with gleeful hauteur, but in reality she felt heavy-eyed. Lifting her fan she hid a yawn behind it.

"I see my warning is already too late."

"Not at all, it's just that it is rather warm ..."

He was going to say something more but

she put her finger to her lips. Dieter was about to sing.

He did indeed have a magnificent voice, but what he sang Liz had no idea; all she heard were waves of sound, like surf on a shore. Her eyes were heavier than ever, so heavy she had to fight to keep them open. Feeling a yawn start she hastily stifled it but heard a smothered laugh, which caused her to jerk upright and apply her fan vigorously.

"You are as high as a kite," Tom murmured.

"I am no such thing, just a little tired, that's all. I had a lot of exercise today."

Too late she realised from his further smothered laughter that she had blundered yet again, not in the least by discovering that he could actually laugh about it.

When Dieter came over to her she was profuse in her praise, though she could not remember a note. She was, however, not so far gone in wine as to accept his offer of a cooling stroll through the gardens. But when he sat down next to her, managing to insinuate a broad arm around her waist, she leaned her head against his massive shoulder and found it wonderfully comfortable. He was murmuring in her ear, but she heard the rumble rather than the words.

Relaxing against him: perhaps if I just close my eyes for a few minutes, she thought ...

When she opened them again it was daylight and she was in her own bed. Shock had her sitting bolt upright, which caused someone to bang a bass drum right by both ears. Wincing, she put her hands over them until the reverberations stopped then carefully turned her head to look at her little travelling clock. It was twelve noon. *Noon!* Oh, my God! It got worse by the hour. She had closed her eyes for a few minutes and gone out like a light!

When she could, Liz slowly and carefully got out of bed to make her equally slow and careful way to the bathroom, where she gritted her teeth and managed to stand for a teeth-chattering whole minute under a very cold shower, after which she slowly increased the heat to a comforting warmth for another five, lathering herself with handfuls of silky foam and washing her hair. By the time she wrapped herself in one of the sheet sized bath towels the drum had been muffled and she felt somewhat better. Two minutes with her electric toothbrush and an extra inch of toothpaste helped even more.

Lowering herself on to the stool in front

of the dressing-table mirror she examined her reflection. She looked no different. No bloodshot eyes, no hang-dog look. Well, it was her very first time. It was also her last if this was how a hangover felt. What *had* she been thinking of? Tom Carey, that's who, she answered herself. The sight of him in elegant black and white had infected her with a fever she had done her best to cool with well-chilled wine, but instead of cooling herself she had no doubt cooled him off. He had warned her, hadn't he? All right, with amusement – a laugh was probably all he would ever manage to raise from now on where she was concerned – but it was a warning nevertheless, which she in her reckless stupidity had ignored. Yet again she had made a fool of herself in front of him. Dressing up to receive, she felt certain, a dressing down. Her sigh weighed a ton, but it was no use sitting here moping. He had to be faced sooner or later. They had planned to leave for London around two o'clock, so she had better get a move on, even if the prospect of spending five hours in a car with him was one she did not relish. Perhaps if she threw herself on the Don's mercy he would mail her back … Moving like a rusty engine she managed to pack, dress and stagger downstairs to the terrace. The sunlight made her clap a hand to her eyes.

"Ah, you are up and about at last, Goddess."

Only the Don sat out, a braille book on his lap.

"Up yes, but I am not yet sure what I am about."

He chuckled. "You have a head, eh? Not surprising. You drank a good deal of champagne last night, and such a hangover can be painful."

"I'll say. If this is a hangover I would rather be hung out to dry. I am sorry to be so late. Is Tom raring to go?"

"He has gone."

Liz felt that like a blow. "Gone!"

"He had to get back, he said, to put matters in hand. I suggested he leave you here with me. After all, you would only have to make the long journey again on Thursday, so I thought it a good idea to let you use these few days peace and quiet to allow you to get on with your painting of the house." The Don held out an envelope. "He left you this."

Liz opened it. A single sheet of paper in Tom's rapid, freestyle hand.

*I know it was a costume party and you entered into the spirit of things with the best of intentions but unfortunately the worst head for liquor. I have to get back to start wheels turning but Il Signore "suggests" you stay behind, and where he is concerned who am I to argue?*
*See you Thursday.*
*Tom*

*P.S. Stick to lemonade in future.*


Liz crumpled the paper in a flare of rage and pain. Lemonade indeed! But her innate honesty made her acknowledge the justice of his observation. In trying to be what she looked, she had remained what she was. Still, there was a crumb of comfort in that he had gone back on his own only because the Don had seen to it that he did.

"I think a cup of hot, fresh coffee," the Don advised.

"I apologise for making a fool of myself."

"But you did not! You merely fell asleep."

"Passed out, you mean."

"You are not used to wine."

"How did I get to bed?"

"Dieter carried you up. Adelina did the rest."

Liz made a strangled sound.

"Dieter was only too happy to assist." The Don had a smile in his voice. "You have got yourself another acolyte."

*Now!* thought Liz. "About Tom ..." she began firmly, as she meant to go on, "it is time I put you straight about him. He is no acolyte of mine. He is very much involved with Melanie, the 'face' of our commercial. You will meet her on Thursday and when you do, Adelina will make you understand why. I know what you have been trying to do but I wish you wouldn't, and in any case it cannot work." It came out in a rush, but it was out.

The Don was silent but Liz pressed on regardless, determined to have her say even if it meant the end of a beautiful friendship. "I know you were only trying to help but if I am ever to get anywhere with my new self then I have to get there on my own, making my own mistakes on the way. Then I will know it is me and not some outside agency who is responsible for the outcome. I know that you have been making Tom aware of me all weekend but really, it has been a waste of time. He—" Liz swallowed— "he does not see me as you would like him to see me; only as a work colleague. At that we do work well together, but outside work his interest is and always has been in Melanie. Their affair is not a new one."

The Don released what sounded like a sigh. "I am sorry," he said regretfully.

"You were not to know. Tom … Tom is an experienced man while I … I am still making my teenage mistakes – like last night, but I am not such an idiot as to make the same mistake twice. Rest assured I learn from each and every one. All I ask of you is that you leave me alone to make them. I will get there in the end, you see if I don't – but on my own."

The Don had been pursing his lips judiciously, now he nodded and said: "I do not doubt it for a moment. Forgive my well-meaning interference. I was, perhaps, too eager to help. You have already come far in a short time. I tremble to think of the effect you will have on men once you have fully gained your confidence as a woman."

Liz leaned forward to squeeze his hand. "You never cease to encourage me."

"I am being factual, merely. Dieter is greatly taken with you. He has gone for a swim – he is a fitness fanatic – but he will be back shortly and I have no doubt he will not leave you alone for long."

Later that morning Liz drove into Falmouth to get herself the materials she needed for her painting, after which she walked the gardens looking for her ideal perspective. After lunch she busied herself with preliminary sketches, only to find herself sitting for long stretches of time staring into space, dissecting that disastrous afternoon and humiliating night, over and over and over again.

# Nine

She awoke on the Thursday morning to the thought that Tom would be arriving but, long though she might to see him, she was terrified at the thought of facing him again, the more so since she knew Melanie would be with him. That was enough to make her decide that discretion was by far the better part of a valour she lacked anyway, and the best thing for all concerned was to absent herself from the villa long before his arrival.

Leaving Dieter and the Don working on Schubert, she took her easel and pad to her selected site: that part of the path from the cliff from which she had first seen the Villa Paradiso. There she became so absorbed that the boom of the luncheon gong startled her. Her instinct was to stay where she was, but experience told her the Don would only send someone to fetch her, so she reluctantly returned to the house.

As she entered the *parterre*, she saw that

184

the terrace seemed to be full of people. Apart from the Don, Adelina and Dieter, Tom was there, along with Dave Barras, the director, an old friend, and the handsome actor who was playing Melanie's Unknown. But it was Melanie who was at the group's centre. She was obviously keeping an eye out for Liz, since as soon as she spotted her she waved and got down from the balustrade on which she was perched, moving to the head of the steps, eager no doubt to point up her porcelain fragility against Liz's sturdy pottery. She was a vision in a drift of band-box fresh summer chiffon; a swirl of cool greens and blues which flattered her skin and hair. Her size three feet were in the highest of cobwebby sandals and her legs were brown and bare, ending in toenails to match the scarlet of those at the ends of her fingers. Liz was at once conscious of her jeans and checked shirt and the fact that the breeze had been at her hair.

"Darling," Melanie trilled, "how disgustingly brown and healthy you look."

"Did you have a good morning?" intervened the Don.

"Yes, thank you. Very satisfactory."

"So was finding this house," Dave Barras said, coming forward to give her a bear hug and a smacking kiss. "If I can't make magic out of this place I don't deserve to be among the world's best ten directors in five years time."

Remembering her manners Liz said a polite hello to Tom, receiving a searching look and a nod in return. She was grateful not to be near him at the luncheon table. She was placed next to Dave Barras, at Adelina's end. Tom and Melanie were seated near their host. Obviously the Don had not only taken Liz's plea to heart, he had acted on it.

"So, how are things with you?" Dave asked. "I have been hearing about you shedding your chrysalis and evolving into a beautiful butterfly."

"All set to shoot these particular segments?" Liz moved him away from a subject she was loathe to discuss with anyone.

"As I will ever be. Your new boss is really uptight about these last segments for some reason. The others were no sweat, and he was no trouble, neither was Her High and Mightiness there, but these last two ... I don't know. Either the campaign is getting to him or she is." Having worked with her too often, Dave had no liking for Melanie.

186

Looking down the table at her, where she seemed to have both the Don and Tom, not to mention Dieter, intent on her every word, he shook his head. "I will never understand how the most intelligent of men can make such fools of themselves over a lovely face."

"You mean you never have?"

Caught by her tone he guffawed so loudly that Tom turned to look, and stayed to watch, but Liz did not see. Her attention was on Dave. One of the things she liked about him was his unfailing sense of humour.

"*Touch*é – it seems we all have the same weakness." Turning in his chair so that he could face her, and thus blocking Tom's view he said, "To get back to what really matters, tell me how you came to find this marvellous place. We are shooting the moonlight segment tonight. Tom was right on the money about that fountain. It is the perfect spot."

After lunch, the crew and their trucks arrived, and they began setting up the lights and the camera. Melanie and her Handsome Unknown disappeared inside their trailers to be made up and dressed ready for lighting, camera and make-up checks while Tom was deep in conversation with Dieter and the Don, seemingly explaining what was going to be done. Liz took advantage of the bustle to slip away and return to her work. When finally she took a break she was satisfied with what she had done so far. She was stretching, flexing her shoulders, when she felt a pair of hands take hold of them and begin to knead, blissfully.

"Thank you, Dieter," she said. "I am rather stiff."

"I can tell. I come to fetch you for dinner, and then we go to watch them film the beauteous Melanie in the light of the setting sun."

"Not me," Liz declined. "I intend to work as long a the light holds out."

"Of course, it must all seem – how you say – old hat, to you, but it is all new to me. I did not know there was so much involved in shooting bits of film that last only seconds."

"Then by all means go and gaze your fill – but not until you have smoothed away the ache below my right shoulder blade – ah, yes, just there ..."

"But what about dinner? Are you not hungry?" Dieter had an appetite to match his size, which was why he worked out so much.

"I brought some fruit. If I want something later I am sure Adelina will not begrudge me a sandwich."

Having previously discovered that once she made a decision she was not easily persuaded to change it, Dieter yielded gracefully. "Whatever you wish," he said, but on giving her painting a more than a cursory glance he leaned over her shoulder to exclaim, "But this is very good! I did not realise you really can paint! How well you have caught the light and shade. I look forward to seeing the final result."

When he left her five minutes later, Liz's shoulders were all loose and pliable again, while her conviction that she had done the right thing had firmed. There was no way she was going to play the masochist and watch Melanie playing not only to an audience, but up to Tom. The Don's 'fee' gave her the perfect excuse. She had casually but deliberately mentioned that she wanted it finished by the time the crew was ready to pack up and return to London, and now that she had Dieter as a witness as to her effort, she sat at it until the light went.

Even then, not until the sun was setting in

a sky that was a blaze of red, gold and several shades of pink and lavender, did she return to the house, entering from the back since she knew they were filming at the front. She met no one on the way, but once safely inside she went to the windows at the top of the main staircase. They gave a panoramic view of the terraces, gardens and fountain, and sure enough, there they all were. Melanie, breathtaking in layers of organza in colours that echoed the sunset, was having her already immaculate hair seen to by her hairdresser, her face by her make-up girl. The Handsome Unknown was likewise being readied. Tom was talking to Dave Barras, gesticulating with his hands at the gardens, while the crew waited, lights, sound and camera at the ready. On the edge of the set, in three chairs, sat the Don, Adelina and Dieter, obviously fascinated by it all.

As she watched, Tom went up to Melanie, now standing ready to go, and said something to her. Slowly, with the absolute confidence of one who knows they are perfection's self, she did a 360 degree turn before facing him again, this time with a smile that to Liz's tortured gaze was one of complicit sexual promise. He nodded, as though to confirm it, then put out a long finger and smoothed away a stray hair caught by the light breeze. In anguish Liz watched as Melanie turned her face into his hand coquettishly before turning away herself, unable to bear any more. The result was that she lay awake for hours and slept badly.

At breakfast next morning, there were only the four of them, since Tom, Melanie, her co-star and Dave Barras were at the Headland Inn, where Liz had first stayed, while the crew were lodged in the village. Liz was quiet, withdrawn, but the Don made a point of saying, "Dieter tells me my painting is coming along nicely."

"Yes, I hope to finish it today. That is why I intend to get an early start."

"Things have gone well here too. Tom tells me they will finish tonight with the full moon shoot so I have decided that after they have – what is it they say: wrapped? – which Tom says should be about half-past nine, I would throw a little party to celebrate, since everything has gone so well. I know Tom is delighted because he told me so."

"Any success will also be due in no small measure to you and this glorious setting.

Thank you again for allowing the agency to use your house." Liz knew she sounded stilted but she could not help it. For some reason she felt like one of her own paint-brushes left to dry without being cleaned first: stiff and breakable.

"Tom has seen to it that the most scrupulous care has been taken at all times. You were right in your summary of his trust-worthiness."

"I am glad it all worked out," Liz said, resolving there and then that since she had nothing to celebrate she would not attend. If they took it for a fit of the sulks so be it, but she knew there was no way she could bring herself to pretend to be happy. If she tried to smile her face would crack. "Now I must go and make good use of all this brilliant sunshine ..."

She stayed away from the house all day. She had told Adelina she would not be in for lunch as she wanted to complete the Don's fee, so had been given half a loaf of *focaccia* spread with *bel paese* and stuffed with Parma ham, a flask of coffee and a bunch of grapes, and nobody came near her while she painted and ate.

By four o'clock she was finished, and well pleased with the result. The house was captured in all its glory, sitting atop its plateau, terraces and gardens falling away below, its walls mellow in the sunshine, its big windows reflecting the light under a sky the colour of the bluebells which grew in profusion in the surrounding woods. All that remained was the proper frame, which she knew she could find at a specialist shop in Islington, then she would give it to Tom who would in turn present it to the Don. What a pity he would never see it except through Adelina's eyes ...

Once more Liz entered the house the back way, using the staircase that led from the kitchen, reaching her bedroom unobserved. There, she carefully propped her painting up to dry, thoroughly cleaned her brushes and put away her paints before taking a leisurely bath, after which she set to work to do a second paint job on herself. Her excuse for non-attendance at the party was a bad headache: too long out in the unshaded sun, would be her line. She knew just how to look the worse for wear. First a pale green cream spread all over her face to give her a deathly pallor, then a delicate grey shadow beneath her eyes. It should be enough to fool Adelina. It would fool me, she thought, as she got into bed. She must have fallen asleep – she had not slept properly since Tom's return – for a knock on her door awoke her. "Come in," she called, her sleep laden voice sounding properly croaky. Expecting a concerned Adelina, she was totally non-plussed when she saw the Don entering.

"Goddess? It is ten o'clock. Are you not coming down to join the festivities?"

"I don't really feel very festive. I think I sat out in the sun too long today, but I did so want to finish your painting …"

Finding her direction by the sound of her voice he came across to sit down on her bed before taking her hand, holding it a moment then saying: "Not hot …" before placing his fingers on her wrist. "A little rapid, but not unduly."

Using the sound of her breathing as his guide he found her face, where he placed a hand on her forehead. "I detect no over-heating," he said. Then in a voice whose gentleness told her he knew what she was up to, "I do not think it is the sun that has struck you down, I think it is the spite emanating from that feline young woman downstairs. You are not going to allow her to outshine you, surely? I thought you had more spirit than that."

194

Liz was silent for a moment before saying flatly, "I am under no illusions as to my own candle when it comes to Melanie's arc-lamp."

"Which she knows and does not hesitate to use to her own advantage. She is quite excited about you, you know, which can only be because she regards you as competition. Were you no threat she would have ignored you, as she does everyone who is of no use to her. Her smile is already the gloat of one who has triumphed, because as far as she is concerned, your absence means that she has. *You must not let her.* Did I not advise you to make your presence felt? It is your presence she fears, believe me. Put on your prettiest dress, come downstairs and outshine her. Will you not relent for me? After the saccharine of Miss Melanie Howard I am in need of something tart and refreshing."

Melanie jealous of *her*, Liz Everett? Liz felt that shot in the arm for the pure adrenaline it was. The Don was an arch-manipulator but he was no liar, and he could read people like his braille books.

"All right," she agreed, spurred by his words into accepting the challenge. "But only for you, and as a means of paying off some of my enormous debt to you."

He had been holding her hand. Now he picked it up to kiss it with a flourish. "That is more my goddess! Come down in all your splendour and make me wish I could see Miss Melanie's face."

Liz got out of bed as the Don was closing her door, only to hear him say, "Yes indeed, my dear Tom. Goddess assures me she will be down shortly. She was resting, merely, after her long day at the easel. Now let us go down to see how things are progressing …" Tom said something else but the door closed, cutting off his words.

Tom had also been coming to find her? Probably to tell her not to sulk, since she had so conspicuously absented herself from everything since his return, and to report for duty at the double. He was still her boss, after all.

Her mood was still a long way from party-like, but taking the Don's words to heart she wiped off her death's head and created a life-enhancing face, using every trick Jilly had taught her, piling her hair high but for a profusion of silky fronds at temples and nape. She set herself adrift on a sea of *Mitsouko* – Melanie would be wearing *L'amoreuse* since her contract stipulated she

196

wear no other perfume – and surveying the finished result decided "If you can't join 'em, beat 'em", going for broke as she donned her purple velvet suit, the colour of which suited her no end, turning her eyes to jade and her skin to clotted cream. Spurred on by her reflection she left undone the top button of her pink organza shirt, thus giving brief but tantalising glimpses of her lace-supported cleavage.

By the time she went downstairs her mood had changed. No longer deep in the slough of despond she was riding the crest of a "ready for anything" wave of combativeness. She found the party in full swing: music playing, champagne-punch flowing, the men outnumbering the women two to one. Apart from herself, and Adelina, there was Marie-Laure, the French *visagiste* who was very Parisian in very chic black, Sandra, the continuity girl, pretty in pink, Kitty, who was Dave Barras's general dogsbody, in sunshine yellow and Annie, Melanie's trusted hairdresser, in soft powder blue. The "star" of their show was still in the glittering Versace dress she had worn for the moonlight shoot, and she was clinging to Tom's arm as if to repel all boarders. He was wearing a beautifully cut pair of dark grey slacks and a thin, silky, champagne-coloured roll-neck sweater under a lightweight jacket. He looked at Liz. She stared coldly back at him until Dave Barras loomed between them.

"At last! But it was worth it! You look gorgeous. Dance?"

"Of course."

The lower terrace had been selected for the dancing, the upper for the food and drink; a sumptuous spread prepared by the help Adelina obtained locally. Leading Liz down the steps Dave proceeded to demonstrate his prowess as a dancer. He might be built like a grizzly bear but he was very light on his feet.

"So, how's the painting coming along?" he asked.

"Finished. That's what I devoted my day to."

"Lucky you. My day was spent being pig in the middle between two people who each wanted their own way."

"Who won?"

"He did, thank God. I'm told he was brought in to handle Melanie and that, I am happy to tell you, is exactly what he does – and beautifully at that. He's got her sussed down to the last pout. I don't mind telling you that if this set of commercials doesn't win an award then I don't know a Leica from a Rolleflex. That was a smashing storyline you wrote – pure romance – and with this location and Melanie's face, the whole series should be a shoo-in for an award."

"I hope so, for your sake."

"Mind you, I did wonder if your absence had anything to do with the *froideur* between you and Carey. You haven't said two words to each other since we got here yet I know he thinks you are the best copy-writer he's ever encountered because he told me so. I wondered why you both came across as two icebergs that pass in the night. I know he's strong-minded, but so are you. What happened – a spat?"

"Yes, of the kind you don't wear with pinstripes."

"Ah ... I thought so. Don't you get on?"

"More like off to bad start."

"You surprise me. He's tough but he's a good bloke and he knows his job. From the reaction of our female complement, who look at him as though they could eat him with a spoon, we should have used him as Melanie's Unknown instead of that hand-some blockhead she insisted on except

199

there's no way she would have tolerated the competition – which is why we got stuck with Noddy, there. The poor sod thinks he's an actor."

He also fancied himself as a ladies man, for as soon as Dave relinquished Liz he was there, and stayed there, until Dieter muscled in. It did Liz a power of good to be claimed to dance again and again, and as the exercise made her glow she took off her velvet jacket, whereupon the sheerness of her organza shirt brightened every male eye.

When eventually she made for the punch bowl on the upper terrace Melanie, who had been watching, narrow-eyed, drifted over to say waspishly, "Making a spectacle of yourself seems to be your stock-in-trade these days, my dear Liz."

Liz froze. The only time she had made a spectacle of herself was the night she had drunk too much and passed out, which meant Tom must have told her. She felt her skin crawl as she imagined them laughing together about it, so her voice was savage when she turned on Melanie, who took an involuntary step back.

"Big spectacles are in right now, haven't you heard? Elton John is not the only one!"

She took her glass of punch over to where the Don, Adelina by his side as always, was sitting in his big chair. Passing Tom on the way she cut him dead. Doing a Melanie and perching on the balustrade by the Don's chair, Liz told him "It is all going extremely well. Everyone is having a whale of time. You were right to persuade me."

"So my 'eyes' tell me. Indeed, the whole thing has been a most enlightening experience. One never ceases to learn and I have learned a great deal, besides being vastly entertained."

"One small – well, twenty-four inches by twenty-four – painting seems a very small price to pay for such kindness. Is there nothing more we can do to show our gratitude?"

"Yes." The Don held out a hand which Liz took. "You can continue to come and visit me whenever you can."

"That is a fee easily paid. You know I would rather come here than go anywhere else."

Just then Adelina murmured something in his ear and still holding Liz's hand he said, "Ah, Tom ... I am just telling my goddess here that it has been a most interesting and enlightening few days. I know you are as pleased as I am with the way things have gone, but then, it was a labour of love was it not?"

Liz had not heard Tom come up behind her, nor did she look at him.

"I don't know about love but the labour came easy. In this place one would expect nothing less. Thank you for allowing me to make it so."

"Goddess here has already thanked me on everyone's behalf. Have you come to ask her to dance? I am told everyone else has."

"The line was a long one," Tom said laconically.

"Then claim your prize." The Don held out Liz's hand to Tom, who was left with no choice but to take it.

"Relax," he advised, as they went down the steps, sensing her mood through the feel of skin on skin. "Let's bury the hatchet – but not in my back, okay?"

She ignored him, gazing steadfastly over his shoulder as he put his arms around her. The music was now slow and sensuous, and she was tall enough for them to be able to dance cheek to cheek. Which, thought Liz fulminatingly, was what he had in full measure. Why would he persist in seeking her out for a little more of the same when he had Melanie parked in a lay-by? As, it seemed, were her own traitorous instincts because as always, his nearness laid long fingers on the knots in which he had her tied and pulled loose every one.

"That's better," he approved. "I am really quite harmless, you know."

"Ha!" scorned Liz. "I have the scars to prove otherwise."

"I would not have to be Count Dracula to want to sink my teeth into that lovely neck of yours, but there have been times when I have been sorely tempted to wring it – ah-ah – no you don't," his grip restrained her from wrenching free. "I am not about to do it here and now so don't take flight."

"Promises, promises," she hissed venomously.

"I never make a promise unless I intend to keep it."

"I'll hold you to that!"

"Just so long as I can go on holding you." As if to demonstrate he pulled her closer. "You are quite an armful."

"You mean Little Red Riding Hood has finally grown up?"

He was silent for a moment then said: "If that particular comment hurt you then I apologise. My justification is that it was said in the heat of the moment, and as moments go it turned into a pretty steamy one ..."

Liz stared fixedly over his shoulder, willing herself not to flush as she remembered his sex growing and hardening against her.

"You keep confusing me with those two identities of yours; one sends out signals the other one refuses to take responsibility for, and I can't get you to tell me why."

"Why should what I feel be any concern of yours?"

He shook her, somewhat impatiently. "Let's not get back on that track again. Adelina has provided lots of delicious goodies, so why keep on stuffing yourself with humble pie? It gives terrible emotional indigestion. You outshine every woman here or do you only believe it when *Il Signore* says so? Was that what he was doing in your room tonight? Working his particular magic?" There was a harsh note to his voice. "Just what is he to you? Sorcerer, Svengali or just plain, old-fashioned sugar-daddy?"

His hand turned into a handcuff as she tried to wrench away. "Temper, temper ..."

"Let me go!" she seethed. "If that is your opinion of me why ask me to dance?"

"*Il Signore* more or less told me I had to."

"Since when did you take orders from a man you don't trust?"

"I am also a practising masochist." The way he said it made her miss a step.

"Let's sue for peace", he suggested after a moment. "What are your terms?"

"Unfriendly!"

He grinned. "Oh, you are on fine form tonight." His voice changed, deepened. "In that shirt and those trousers, very fine form indeed."

Liz blushed. He was flirting again. What was he trying to do? Lead her down the garden path? When she knew all too well that there were only theories at the bottom of it.

"You are the only woman I know who can do that," he marvelled as she rosied up, in a way that had her responding unthinkingly, "You are the only man who can make me."

"Now why is that, I wonder?"

She lowered her lids over her eyes before the look in his. His laugh was short. "Oh, yes, you are learning." Was that regret she heard? "To get back to our lamentable state of hostilities: can I sue for peace? Name your terms."

"Unconditional surrender!" Too late Liz realised where her always quick-on-the-draw tongue had led her, producing another mortified flush.

"Any minute now you'll go up in flames!" he said, but there was definitely tenderness colouring his amusement, "and for God's sake! don't look at me like that! I am only human and can stand only so much. I'd rather you gave me the serrated edge of your tongue." He pulled her even closer. "Let's just dance," he commanded, sounding desperate, and as if whoever was operating the CD player heard him, the music changed, slowing to something that picked them up and wrapped them in it. She felt his lips graze her ear. "You smell intoxicating. What – or who – changed your mind about that?"

*You*, she thought, unable to tell him. Desperately she reached for a club with which to fend him off. "Why did you tell Melanie I made a spectacle of myself?"

He looked surprised. "Why should you think I would?"

"But she said—"

"Melanie says a great many things, most of which are to gain an advantage, but at least now I have an explanation for the frozen mitt you threw at me earlier. Melanie, you innocent, is jealous!"

Exactly what the Don had said, so it had to be true.

Tom shook his head wonderingly. "You just don't realise just exactly what you are, do you?"

But Liz was staring, entranced, at the picture of Melanie being jealous of her former pet elephant. It was not until she heard him say, "Let's kiss and make up, shall we?" that she came out of her reverie to find he had danced her to the far end of the terrace where the spreading blossom of a big lilac tree made for a cave of deep shadow. Before she knew what he was about he was kissing her again. Liz forced herself to wrench her head away, determined not to go down that road again: she'd been knocked down once already.

"No – it's not right – I don't want ..."

"Yes, yes, you do. All your signals are green ..."

He captured her chin, and turning her face to him kissed her again, and it was like it had been on the beach: desperate, wild, as though they could not get enough of each other. He kissed her deeply and passionately and, opening his jacket, Liz put her arms around him, feeling his warmth, pressing herself against him. He ran his hands down her body, drawing her hips against his hardness. Liz made a sound deep in her throat which had him trailing his lips down it to her shirt, which he unbuttoned, along with the front fastening of her lace bra. His mouth was hot, greedy, and she shivered as it scorched her skin. In a thick, hoarse voice he said, "I take it back – Little Red Riding Hood was never like this. It is some place, this Olympus of yours, the Greeks certainly did have a word for it but right now I can't think what it was … I can't get my mind around anything but you …"

Liz was not capable of thinking either, only feeling.

When the scream came it was such that they sprang apart like a busted spring.

"What the hell?" Tom scowled furiously, turning to look, then suddenly he was off and running to where a group of people were bending over something – *someone* – lying at the foot of the flight of steps leading to the lower terrace.

# Ten

Running after him, as she neared the group Liz saw that it was Dave Barras who was bending while Adelina was kneeling by the side of an inert figure sprawled head first down the last four steps. It was the Don. And it was Melanie, standing over him, who was screaming hysterically. Shoving her aside so impatiently she stopped in mid peal, Tom bent over the Don to demand, "What happened?"

Dave Barras said, "He was going down the steps with Melanie when suddenly he tripped and fell – all the way to the last four."

"But he knows these steps!" Liz heard her own voice say. "He goes up and down them umpteen times a day and I have never seen him so much as falter!"

"Not this time. He tripped, I tell you. I saw him stumble."

Tom lifted one of the Don's eyelids. "He's

unconscious. Somebody had better call an ambulance. *Now!*"

Glad to be able to do something Liz pushed her way through the silent cluster at the top of the steps and ran to the telephone in the Don's study where she dialled 999 and requested an ambulance urgently, giving full details of the address and the details of the accident. Then she raced upstairs to her bedroom where she pulled both duvet and pillows from her bed, hazily remembering that in cases of shock, warmth was essential. On running back to the terrace with them she found that Sandra, a qualified First Aider, had taken charge. Spreading the duvet over the Don she shook her head at the pillows. "Best not to move him in any way. He has a head injury." Which was when Liz saw the blood seeping from it onto the stone. Melanie had obviously thrown herself at Tom because she was in his arms, crying hysterically, repeating that it was not her fault; that she had only meant to dance with him ... and she had been holding his hand oh, so carefully ...

Through her dread and shock and the wail of Melanie's hysterics Liz became conscious of another voice, that of Adelina, spitting forth a tirade of Italian. Not understanding a word Liz looked down at her bewilderedly. She was still kneeling at the Don's side but pointing, dramatically and with a shaking forefinger, to the fourth step. Protruding from the ornamental balustrade was a length of cable that had been overlooked in the crew's clearing away, and over it lay the Don's shoe.

"Oh, dear God, no!"

At Liz's gasp Adelina turned on her, and in a welter of Latin emotionalism proceeded to direct another spate of Italian at her of which nobody understood a word, mixed with English everyone understood only too well.

"Your fault! All your fault! You bring these people here! No good for him, you. A young girl and an old, blind man! Look you! Half naked! *Desgrazia! Svergignato!*"

Liz needed no translation for those last two words. *Disgrace! Shameless!* Then she noticed where Adelina was directing her gaze, and looking down saw her shirt gaping where Tom had undone the buttons as well the front fastening of her Wonderbra, exposing her naked breasts. Colour flooded her face a dull, humiliated red before leaching away to whiteness as

211

she hastily covered herself.

"Yes, cover yourself. Shameless, you! You not wanted here. Bad things happen because of you. Better you go. Go!"

Before Tom could free himself from Melanie Liz had fled.

It was Dieter who eventually found her, in the yew arch, which he had already passed and re-passed. This time, thinking to look inside he peered in and saw her in the shadows, curled up on the wooden bench, knees drawn up against her chest, arms around them, face buried in them.

"At last! I have been looking everywhere for you. There is hot coffee for everyone. Come and have some. Tom has gone to the hospital in the ambulance with the Don, but he told me to find you and make sure you were all right. I have searched these gardens twice."

She did not answer, and when he looked closer he saw that her face was blank and her eyes unfocused. He said something in German that sounded violent. "You must not worry over what Adelina said. She is Italian; emotional and hot tempered. I know her for some time now and she is very protective of *Il signore*. It was because she was afraid he was perhaps going to die that she made such a scene. Come, let us go back to the house. There is not much point in sitting here in the dark, is there?"

Talking to her cajolingly he got her to her feet and back to the house, avoiding the low-voiced group on the terrace. He took her up to her room, where he sat her down on her bed. Leaving her there he went back downstairs again and seeking out Sandra, explained the situation as he took her up to Liz.

"Shock," was her verdict. "Go downstairs and bring back a cup of hot, sweet tea. And see if you can find some sort of a sedative somewhere – oh, and you had better bring that duvet back, not to mention the pillows. They obviously came from here."

She was a bossy little thing, Dieter thought as he went downstairs, but pretty with it.

Liz had neither moved nor spoken by the time Dieter came back, bearing the duvet and pillows under one arm and carrying a tray with the other on which were a large mug of tea and a bottle of green pills. "I found these in the bathroom cabinet in the Don's room. I know he sometimes has trouble sleeping so they must be the pills he takes." Sandra took the bottle, read the label and nodded. "Yes, one of these will give her twelve hours sleep, all right." She shook a pill into her palm, handed the bottle back to Dieter and said briskly, "You can put it back where you found it. Thanks for your help. I can manage the rest."

Sandra made Liz open her mouth, popped the pill inside and then coaxed her to drink the hot, sweet tea, which she did without seeming to be conscious of it, for normally she never took sugar, after which Sandra undressed her and put her to bed, leaving the dressing table lamp lit, moving it so that it did not shine in her eyes.

"Things will look better in the morning," she soothed as she left. *I hope to God*, she thought, crossing her fingers just in case.

When Tom got back to the villa it was almost two a.m. and he found that everyone and everything had gone. There were no vans, no trucks, no big catering Winnebago, no party debris, no people. The villa was quiet and deserted but for Dave Barras, who had remained behind to put him in the picture.

"How is the old man?" he asked Tom.

"A skull fracture, with some intercranial bleeding. He is in Intensive Care and

214

Adelina insisted on staying behind with him. I'm to ring in the morning for a progress report. What happened here? Where's Liz? Is she all right?"

"Dieter found her in the gardens in a state of – shock, I suppose. Not surprising considering the way that Italian virago let loose. Shades of Anna Magnani! And to Liz, of all women! Which also means, knowing her as I do, that her over-developed sense of duty has no doubt taken on board all the blame for tonight's little fiasco, seeing as she was the one who set the whole thing in motion."

"No, she didn't. I did."

"She won't see it that way."

"Where is she now?"

"Sandra put her to bed with a sleeping pill then everybody pitched in and cleared away – we even washed the dishes – after which, by general consensus, there was a general exodus. There was nothing more we could do, after all. Melanie went back with Noddy, not very pleased that you abandoned her – that was the way she put it. She seemed to think she should have been your first concern. Mine was to find out how the hell that cable came to be overlooked, so I had a word with the electrician. He told me

215

that what tripped the old man was a short extension, which he thinks must have parted from the main cable when they were packing up and fallen between the steps and the yew hedge at the side. He was gutted, I can tell you."

"So he damned well should be. It was sheer carelessness. I only got the use of this house through Liz and I gave my word to its owner that we would take every possible care in return for that use. Now he's in Intensive Care and Liz is in a state of shock after being branded a whore by a woman who knows enough to know better! What's his explanation for the cable finding its way through the balustrade?"

"The constant movement of human traffic both on the upper terrace, and up and down the steps during the course of several hours. That probably caused it to creep its slow way through the pilasters of the balustrade. I was up and down umpteen times and I didn't see it."

"I still intend to hold an inquest once this thing is settled."

"That is your prerogative, but now that you are back I'll follow the others." Dave paused. "Apart from tonight, this was a dream of a shoot. I'll have a rough cut for

216

you as soon as I can, probably by the time you get back yourself. Okay?"

Tom nodded.

Dave tried again. "Look, Liz is a strong girl with a lot of common sense – I know you had to go with the Don, and she won't blame you for that ... she got a nasty shock, that's all—"

Tom cut him off. "I am aware of that." *And a lot else besides*, he thought, *about which you know nothing*: like Liz's vulnerability right now. That Adelina should turn on her so viciously had thrown them all for a loop, what it had done to Liz God alone knew, except that it had hit her where it hurt most. His instinct had been to follow her when she fled the scene, but his duty had been to stay and deal with the situation. Which he had done to the best of his ability. Still, it just went to show how deep still waters like Adelina's did run. Always so calm and controlled on the surface, but underneath a boiling mass of jealousy. His sigh was heavy. Tonight's display of it from one woman to another could not have come at a worse time, on top of a tragic accident to the one man with the power to undo them both.

When he went upstairs to check on Liz he

found her deeply asleep, lying on her back like a tomb effigy. He stood looking at her for a long time, before running his hands through his hair frustratedly and uttering an explosive "Shit!" after which he went back downstairs.

Dieter was in the kitchen, sitting at the big butcher-block table with a glass and a bottle of whisky. Seeing Tom he reached for another glass and poured a double. "You need this, I think."

"Do I not!"

Refilling the glass Tom emptied Dieter asked, "So, what do they say about my Maestro?"

"Is that what you call him?"

Dieter's grin was knowledgeable. "Somehow I do not think you would, but he is my teacher, even if I am the only pupil in his Master Class."

Tom levelled a look. "So, can you tell me how he and Melanie came to be descending those steps when he fell."

Dieter shrugged. "She saw you dancing with Liz and did not like it. That was the first thing. Then when she looked again you had both disappeared. That was the second thing. It was obvious she was not happy about that, not happy at all. I think the

Maestro was trying to divert her by offering to dance with her himself. He does it very well, you know, even if he is blind."

"Did he know what was happening?"

A shrug. "Adelina tells him *everything*." Leaning forward slightly as if to emphasise what he was about to say, Dieter continued, "Let me tell you about my Maestro and Adelina. There is an aria in *Don Giovanni* which says, in effect, *my peace depends upon yours, your sigh is my sigh, what pleases you is my happiness, what hurts you gives me pain and there is no joy for me unless you share it.* That is how Adelina sees him. That is why she was so – upset."

"Upset! She went ape!" Tom paused. "Had she reason to be?"

Dieter looked affronted. "That is not his way. With Liz he was never anything but fatherly. He introduced her to me as his god-daughter."

"He has enormous influence over her, nevertheless." Tom paused again. "How well do you know him?"

"Since three years. He was – is – a great singer and has taught me much. He is a great teacher." Now it was Dieter's turn to pause. "Of more than singing, I think." Dieter poured them both some more whisky before asking idly: "Will you stay here tonight?"

"If it is permitted."

Dieter shrugged again. "Who is to say no? But let us finish this bottle of whisky first."

Tom pushed his glass forward.

# Eleven

When finally he went upstairs he found Liz lying as he had left her. Such a big girl with a little girl's vulnerability. A complex bundle of contradictions and unexpected joys, who played a defensive game against life, never straying far from her well-defended position and lobbing deadly accurate verbal barbs at the first sign of danger. He only hoped this lousy night had not sent her behind those defences for good, because Dave had her bang to rights. She would blame herself for it.

Drawing the duvet around her he smoothed her hair back from her forehead. It felt like silk and still smelled heady. Another sign of her bid for recognition. About which he had signally – and frustratedly – failed to get her to come clean. Probably because it had everything to do with that blind man, who had such a hold over her. It was obvious he was behind her

221

transformation because it was after a visit to this – *his* – paradise that she had begun to come out from under. How had he managed it; more important, *what were his reasons for managing it?*

Tom had not been aware of her complexities at first; not even been aware of her except as the name behind some of the best copy he'd ever read. To familiarise himself with the style of his new agency, he had gone through its earlier campaigns, only to become aware that the memorable ones all had the same copy signature. Elizabeth Everett. When he had asked who and where she was they had said she was in Australia with the boss, establishing the fledgling Australian agency.

"She stands out," he had commented, meaning her work, and wondered why they had smiled, deciding it meant that her looks matched her talent,. He had therefore been more than curious to meet her, only to find that the vintage champagne copy had been written by a big, homely, iced-tea girl in what he took to be a maternity dress, but on enquiring if she was indeed pregnant they had looked at him blankly. "Liz lives with and for her job," he was informed.

Relieved that he was not about to lose the

best copy-writer he'd ever encountered, he also found his curiosity aroused, since he could not reconcile the memorable copy with the instantly forgettable appearance, especially when he realised, during the course of several discussions with her, that she spoke as she wrote.

The dichotomy intrigued him, caused him to speculate as to the reasoning behind it. Like why she did not try to conceal her personality, which was memorably distinctive; tartly flavoured, with a tongue like a buzz-saw and a mind like an Intel processor with four gigabytes of RAM, yet concealed her physical self under pup-tents and presented a soap-and-water face which said: This is how I am. Take me or leave me. He wondered if perhaps she had difficulty dealing with her sexuality until he realised that she dressed as she did because she did not believe she had any, since she had absolutely none of the gestures, inflexions or body movements of a woman open to offers from men. Which was when he realised something else: she never expected any.

Further casually planted questions among the staff brought forth the fact that she was a loner who did not join in any of the office parties or get-togethers, except for the obligatory Christmas Cocktail bash. She and her group lunched together every day at a nearby *trattoria*, but that was because she was regarded as one of the guys; "a good bloke" as they said over here. Never, ever as a desirable woman.

And then he discovered that Melanie regarded Liz Everett as her personal punching bag; came to realise, on listening to Beauty denigrating the Beast, that the poor Beast hated itself for Melanie's shortcomings. So he encouraged Melanie's chatter, which made her happy since it reinforced her devout narcisism, and because it turned out to be highly informative, enabling him after some more DIY psychoanalysis to diagnose the source of the Everett trouble as an Everest-sized inferiority complex. This was confirmed when Liz retreated at the first sign of more than impersonal interest on his part. Bad experience, he decided, after developing Melanie's negatives into a full-colour ten by ten, had led Liz Everett to the view that there had to be an angle, and she would inevitably be the one to end up hanging from it.

Far from being satisfied at his explanation, his curiosity had turned rogue. Which was when he decided to do something about her, (a) because he liked her and (b) her current, enclosed convent-like existence was a criminal waste of an unusual woman. He had made up his mind to give it a try when he had the time, since Melanie was a full-time job, what with the campaign and all, but by the time he was both ready and able, Liz had gone away for a week and when she came back he saw he had left it too late. He had been right on the money where she was concerned but somebody – some man, he thought frustratedly – had got there first.

When he saw her in the restaurant that night it was like being punched in the gut, and it was no consolation to see that his sixth-sense instincts about her had been right even if his timing had been way off. Under the burlap was the most abundant of women; all creamy flesh and slumberous sexuality, innocently displayed by one who obviously had no idea of its effect. Somebody had beaten him to it, all right, but who? Not the man she was with; he had the scorch-marks of a man well and truly singed but not the potency of the man who had brought about this incredible metamorphosis of a woman who had refused to acknowledge she was one. He had determined to find out, but by then the competition was fierce, so he had made it his business to drop in on the After Six Club, and knew he had found his man when he saw her sketch of this villa and heard her speak of her "friend".

Tom saw at once that here was his means of introduction to where he wanted to go. That it was also perfect for his working needs was an added bonus, but to find out that Liz's Svengali was not only blind but old enough to be her father had been a tough call. Until he worked out the all important why. It was *because* he was blind. He had not been able to see what she was but *he had sensed what she could be*, and because of that she had been able to open up to him, tell him the things she could not bring herself to tell a man with eyes, like his own, for instance, because too many men's eyes had looked and not seen.

To find that her sorcerer was also a skilled interpreter of people had been Tom's second strike. He might not be able to see faces but boy, could he ever read voices and the things they did not say. Which had to be why he had Liz laid out like a detailed story-board. From things that were said, Tom had deduced that the Don, as Liz called him, had convinced her that far from being the Little Miss Reject of Melanie's taunting, she was worth any man's second glance but only if she was prepared to throw off her disguise. And it had worked – up to a point. Because it seemed she was having a hard time believing it, since at the first sign of his own interest she was all defensive prickles, with the result that they had become embroiled in one slanging match after another.

The Don, of course, had as the Brits said, "sussed" him out at once, hence his manipulation of every situation, to Liz's obvious embarrassment and his own fury. But those machinations had led to him confirming one thing for sure. Liz's response to him was all his atavistic, hunting-male instincts had told him from the very beginning they could be. Under the controlled exterior was a fiery core, though she was clearly an emotional and physical virgin, which was why she could not bring herself to let go. Yet it was those same inexperienced blunders which had endeared her to him in a way that caught at him as no other woman's more experienced responses had ever done, and in twenty-years as a practising heterosexual he had been around the block a few times. It was Liz's inability to deal with what happened on the river that had driven her to flirt with that hulking German, only to drink herself into oblivion.

He had planned to have it out with her on the drive back to London, but the wily old fox had blackmailed him into leaving her behind, and on his return with the crew she had backed off so far she had been out of sight, ostensibly busy with that damned painting.

Tonight, Tom realised, holding up his own actions to the light and examining them for errors and/or omissions, had been the action of a desperate – and jealous – man. Determined on a showdown, he had gone upstairs to flush her out, only to find the Don coming out of her room. And when she had finally appeared, she had undermined his every resolution so badly he had fallen through them, for the beautiful creature in the purple velvet trouser suit was light years removed from the drab Liz Everett who had told him with flippant bitterness than she was going to Paradise. Never had he hated the Don so much, with the result that resentment had screwed him to such a pitch he had gone and created a situation which had led to a disaster, causing Liz to take not only physical but emotional flight in the belief that the mob was combing the gardens with torches.

Damn Melanie and her jealousy, and thank God this campaign was now in the can and she was off his back. That had been his remit. Whatever *she* wants until she gives us what *we* want – this time. By the time we are ready for another television campaign she will be over the hill and the client will be ready for a change. She had picked up on his interest in Liz, of course. Where that sort of thing was concerned she saw further than the Hubble telescope. Well, it made no mind now. What mattered was that he should be here when Liz came to, so that he could put things right between them, especially since she would not have the Don to turn to.

Shedding his jacket, Tom loosened his collar and kicked off his shoes. Then he drew up the big armchair by the bed, near enough so that he could prop his feet on it, settling a cushion behind his head and spreading the spare blanket over him. He probably wouldn't sleep much, he reasoned, but three double scotches would ensure that he got some rest, because tomorrow would bring either rescue or disaster.

Birdsong woke him, and he got up with a crick in his neck and stiff shoulders. Stretching hugely he felt his muscles crack. Bending over Liz he saw she had not so much as moved, so he went downstairs to the telephone. Mr diMarco's condition was stable, he was informed, but since there was evidence of a sub-dural haematoma they had decided to operate to relieve pressure. He was being prepared for surgery even as they spoke If Mr Carey would like to ring back at around noon ...

Tom set coffee to drip then went outside to see what the weather was like, to find it had changed: it was cloudy and the breeze was chill. He hoped to God it was not an omen.

He was drinking coffee when Dieter came down. "You are an early riser," he observed, sounding surprised. "I come down to do my morning fifty laps then I will have breakfast. If you wish to have some I will cook for us both."

"I'll go back upstairs to shower and change first."

"How is Liz?"

"Still sleeping." He told Dieter the news from the hospital.

"He is strong for an old man," Dieter said confidently.

"Strong yes, old no."

Dieter flicked him a look but said nothing more.

Finding his bag, which Dave Barras had left behind, Tom shaved, showered and changed before looking in on Liz again. She was still asleep, so with another cup of coffee in his hand he went back to the phone and called the agency. John Brittan was not there, but "Uncle" Fred Barnes was, so Tom explained the situation to him, minus Adelina's outburst and Liz's reaction, accepting full responsibility and promising to ring back as soon as he had any further news.

"Will he sue, do you think?" Fred asked anxiously.

*Not if it concerns Liz,* Tom thought, before answering. "He does not strike me as the kind of man who reaches for his lawyer at the first sign of trouble."

"Well, if he does we have a case against the film company. It was their employee who overlooked that piece of cable after all."

"Let's see what the hospital has to say after he has been operated on," Tom said.

231

"Conjecture is of no help right now."

"True, true ... I leave everything in your capable hands, Tom. Keep me informed – and regards to Liz."

While Dieter was cooking bacon, eggs, tomatoes and mushrooms and toasting what looked like half a loaf, Tom went back upstairs again, anxious to be there when Liz awoke, but she was lying exactly as he had left her. So he went back downstairs for some breakfast.

Liz was just surfacing, as from a deep, black well, when the soft "click" of her bedroom door brought her to instant alertness. She did not move, but lifted her lashes a fraction to see Tom Carey come in through it.

She made herself breathe quietly and regularly until, after what seemed the longest moment of her life, she heard her door close again. Letting go a long, shaky breath she lay back on her pillows. Tom was the last person she was up to facing because memory, flooding back with the daylight, blurrily replayed last night's scene: Adelina's raging condemnation, her own half-naked dishevelment, the avidly watching spectators, but worse, oh God, worst of

232

all ... the Don lying on the ground, blood seeping from his head. She had to get to him. But where was he? He was not a young man after all. In addition to his head injury he could have broken bones; an arm, a leg, God alone knew. He could even be dead. Whatever he was she had to find out.

Throwing back the duvet she got up, discovered she was in bra and briefs, but had no memory of being put to bed. No memory of anything after fleeing the scene. Truth to tell everything seemed rather thick and opaque, as though she had just swum up from the darkest of depths to encounter, just below the surface, a patch of clinging weeds that prevented her from surfacing. She could see light, but somehow was not able to break through to it. A shower, she thought. She also scrubbed her teeth to rid herself of the sickly sweet taste in her mouth and drank two glasses of cold water. When she was dressed, her hair was damp but she had no time to dry it. Picking up her shoulder bag she went carefully and silently downstairs.

There was no sign of anyone. Making her way to the back of the house she felt thirsty again, and decided another glass of cold water would not go amiss, but as she neared the kitchen she heard a voice. Tom. Obviously on the telephone, because he would speak, then there would be a silence then he would speak again. Perhaps he was enquiring about the Don. Creeping forward she stealthily pushed open the swing door an inch or two so as to eavesdrop.

"... No, I'll stay put until I know exactly how things stand. I have to call the hospital – in Falmouth – to see how the operation went. Hopeful, was the word they used, but still a case of quickest done soonest mended. No, nobody else, the crew left last night ... there's only Liz and me here now. What? I'll give you three guesses ... right! A grandstand tantrum, what else? It was all her damned fault anyway, leading that old man on."

Liz first recoiled, then turned and staggered away, feeling she had been kicked in the stomach. She had no memory of throwing a tantrum. She had been upset, yes. She remembered her devastating feelings of shame and embarrassment after Adelina had not spared her, but she remembered nothing after turning tail. All right, so she was a coward, but hysterics had never been her style. Well, at least now you know, she told herself bleakly. It was indeed no more than a try-on on his part. He believes you are having an affair with the Don and because of that, you would not be averse to distributing your favours in his direction.

That she was far removed from her normal clarity of thought, or that her very thought processes were clogged by the residue of the powerful sleeping pill she had been given, did not occur to her. She only knew she felt betrayed by Tom Carey, and in self-defence all her instincts rushed to concentrate on one thing: the Don. She had to get to him, explain to him. Yes. That was the most important thing. Get to him. Tell him how bitterly she regretted bringing Tom and everything and everybody connected with that damned commercial down to Cornwall, disrupting his peaceful retirement.

It had been a bad mistake on her part, and she needed desperately to be able to look at him while she begged him to forgive her for making it; to plead with him not to turn her out of his life ... which would happen anyway if he died ... No! She killed that thought, but just in case it would be as well to get to him – *now!*

Without further thought she left the house, and once in the gardens took to her

235

heels to reach the Inn on the headland, where she asked the landlord about a taxi to Falmouth.

When it dropped her outside the entrance to the hospital, she entered Reception on the run, only to be told that Mr diMarco was still in the recovery room, and that Signora Rinaldi, who had brought him in, had been waiting all night.

Liz went down the corridor to where a sign said WAITING ROOM – VISITORS ONLY and through the big windows, saw Adelina huddled in a chair, her arms wrapped about her body, rocking backwards and forwards in silent keening, suffering dark eyes staring at nothing. As Liz entered the room she looked up and their eyes met. At once a spasm of conflicting emotions passed rapidly across Adelina's drawn face. They graphically told Liz that while she was fearfully afraid for the Don, she was also terrified that Liz would tell him what had been screamed at her over his prostrate body. There was desperate entreaty in the dark eyes as they silently beseeched Liz to understand before Adelina hid her face in her hands, bursting into sobs as she did so.

"Please ... you not tell what I say ...

things not meant ... such fear for him, you understand ... I am upset and afraid ... how you say ... *geloso*."

"Jealous?"

"*Si* ... I know he love you, but – *cual figlia* – you understand?"

"Like a daughter?"

Adelina nodded vigorously. "*Si ... si ...*" Then, the wet, velvety eyes still desperate with a mixture of fear and pleading, she repeated, "You not tell him, please ... he have much anger ... truly I not mean what I say ... I am afraid he die ... I know what I say not true, but my fear and jealousy make me say wild things. Please, you forgive and not tell him ... he will send me away and I have no life without him. Please, I beg of you ... be kind ... forgive and forget."

"Of course I will not tell him." Liz binned her intention to set the record straight since Adelina had now rendered the need obsolete. "But how is he? Have they told you anything?"

"Something press inside his head ... they cut ..." Adelina scissored her fingers then buried her face in her hands again. "I fear for him ... and for myself. He is my life. If he die, I die ... that is why I say these bad things to you ..."

"He won't die," Liz said fiercely. "We must not even think that."

Adelina managed a small smile, then timidly she held out a hand. Liz took it and thus they sat, holding on by the simple means of holding hands, until a doctor came to tell them the good news that the operation had been a success: the pressure had been relieved, the bleeding stopped. The Don was resting comfortably but they would not be able to see him for some time yet.

Adelina, who had been listening intently, eyes wide, hands clasped as though in prayer, heard the magic words "success" and "resting comfortably" then, crossing herself fervently, burst into another torrent of Italian, this time including the names of various saints and that of the Blessed Virgin, after which she again threw her arms around Liz when she attempted to restore calm, begging her once again to forgive her and say nothing to *Il Signore*.

"I have told you, not a word," Liz said, which had Adelina embracing her once more. She was all but composed again, mopping tears from a now radiant face with eyes once more showing signs of life, when a kindly nurse brought them both a cup of tea before asking Liz: "Are you Miss Everett?"

"Yes. Why?"

"A Mr Carey just telephoned, asking about Mr diMarco, and when I told him the news he enquired about the Italian lady. I told him you were with her and he asked me to tell you he was on his way."

Tom! In her over-riding fear for the Don, all other considerations had gone by the board. Now that he was safe, Liz felt her sense of betrayal regain consciousness and let go a scream of agony. Her ego had been stabbed in its most tender part, forcing her to limp back to her previous existence as this or any other year's Queen of the Rejects. He had shown his true feelings by listening to Adelina screaming abuse at her and doing nothing to contradict her because it was obviously what he too believed. He had not even come looking for her when she fled. No, he had stayed with Melanie, holding *her* in his arms and comforting *her*. Not until this morning had he bothered about Liz.

And it was not as if she did not know how men said one thing and thought another. Sharing a flat with three other girls for almost a year had been a sentimental education, the means of her learning – second hand but nevertheless taken to heart – of the casual betrayals perpetrated by men when in pursuit of their aim – invariably the same one – to get the object of their pursuit between the sheets. Since all three girls were in and out of relationships like yo-yos, Liz had been privy to the tears, the lacerated sensibilities, the broken hearts, the betrayed trusts and dumped miseries – except for Melanie, whose heartless beauty had ensured she always had the upper hand. But Penny and Grace, both attractive though not in Melanie's league, had showed Liz that men would tell any lie, commit any act, to get what they wanted. It had seemed to Liz, watching and listening from the sidelines, that their desire had more to do with what they carried between their legs than in their hearts. Now, she had her own proof. What Tom Carey had said and done, especially last night, was as big a lie as any uttered to Penny and Grace, but at least she had not, as both girls had sobbed – "gone to bed with the bastard".

She had thought she would feel anger, be ready to rend and tear, but she felt nothing, only empty and very heavy hearted. Even so, by the time Tom entered the waiting room thirty minutes later, her nerves were wound so tightly they threatened to cut off her emotional circulation. His gaze was searching, but as he saw her and Adelina sitting together and took in the situation, his tense expression cleared somewhat. He spoke first to Adelina, in her own language, bending down to her and taking the hands she held out.

Whatever he said was the right thing because Adelina's smile was radiant and her answer a happy one, but then she spoke rapidly and anxiously to him at some length, and the glance he flicked at Liz told her what it was about. When finally he turned to her, he said, "Why didn't you ask me to drive you here? I was worried when I went to check on you and found your bed empty. Are you all right?"

"I am fine, and I have no wish to be any *more* trouble to you," Liz answered pointedly.

"Since when have you ever been anything else?" he asked, but humorously, and with a smile that faded as he got absolutely no response.

"Are you sure you are all right?" he asked, his frown one of concern. "I realise that the events of last night must have come as a

241

nasty shock in more ways than one, but thank God things have ended far better than any of us could have hoped, as I have just learned. There is nothing to be done here now except wait. Why not come back to the villa with me. He is out of danger now."

"I am not leaving here until I have seen him," Liz said, in a flat voice. "It does not matter how long I have to wait. He is all that matters to me right now. Do I make myself clear?"

She saw his face change. "What's wrong?" he demanded.

"Don't be stupid," Liz derided.

Equally cold, Tom said, "It seems I have been."

"Then we have both learned a lesson, haven't we?"

"Can't we talk about this?"

"Why?"

"You know damned well why!"

Liz looked straight at him. "Yes, I do," she agreed, "which is why I have nothing to say to you, now, or ever." She could see he was furious, knew he was utterly taken aback, but felt no pity. Felt nothing. Only the wish that he would go away and leave her alone. Which he did.

When he had gone, Liz felt Adelina's

other hand cover hers, looked at her, met a pair of agonised, penitent dark eyes, and against her will, felt her own fill and spill. She wanted to howl, to scream, to do something to relieve her sudden flare of pain, but she only bit hard on her lip instead.

"Is all my fault ..." Adelina whispered. *"Dio Mio!* What have I done?"

"Brought me to my senses," Liz answered raggedly. "No!" she shook her head as Adelina went to say more. "I don't want to talk about it."

Adelina subsided, but from the look on her face it was unhappily. It was two o'clock before they were allowed to see the Don, out of Recovery and in his own room in the private wing. His face was colourless beneath a turban of bandages, but his breathing was even and steady. His condition was stable, they were told, his pulse strong, and he had come through the operation well. He was resting comfortably and once out of hospital – hopefully in about ten days or so – it would be no more than a case of rest and care. They were advised to go home and get some rest themselves. They could return the following day, when the Don would be fully conscious and able to talk to them.

Having seen for herself that he was indeed safe, Adelina agreed to return to the villa to get some sleep, so they got a taxi back. Dieter met them, having been told the good news by Tom, who had returned briefly to collect his bag before leaving to take the good news back to London. The way Liz looked had Dieter eyeing her doubtfully, but he said nothing. Obviously something had gone very wrong. Tom had also looked grim, his clipped responses to questions likewise preventing Dieter from asking what it was.

Next morning, the Don was awake, but drowsy. He listened to them smilingly but said little, yet Adelina told Liz happily later that his grip on her hand was firm when he raised it to his lips. They learned that Mr Carey had called in on his way back to town the day before and taken a full report of the Don's condition back with him.

Liz did not return to London. Instead she rang John Brittan and asked for leave of absence due to the prevailing circumstances, which he gladly gave. She ought to have called Tom by rights, as he was her Creative Director, but she had no compunction in going over his head. In any case, she had no desire to speak to him.

Each day they visited the Don he was stronger, and after a week he was sitting up and talking as if nothing had happened. He waved aside Liz's abject apology. "It was not your fault," he said. "Adelina has explained about the cable, and I have heard from Tom, who accepts full responsibility."

"But—" She had rehearsed an explanation as to why Tom was there and she was here but she did not get to give it.

"No buts, Goddess. It is over and I would prefer it to be done with." It was an order, but one she concurred with.

On the Sunday afternoon, Adelina, Liz and Dieter, who this time had come with them after being warned by Liz to say nothing about Adelina's outburst, were kept waiting before being admitted to see the Don as the doctors were with him. Nothing untoward, they were assured, merely a routine examination.

When finally they were allowed into his room they found him in an upbeat mood and wearing dark glasses. "These are to help the slight headache I have developed; a side-effect of the operation which will go in time. They assure me it is nothing to worry about."

He talked happily of going home, of

celebrating his return with a party. He also told them that he had again talked to Tom. "Do you know he has called every day to enquire about my progress? And he – or rather the agency – is paying for all this?" He waved a hand around his luxurious private room, the flowers decorating it, the get well cards ranged on top of the chest of drawers. "I have had cards from everyone … so kind. You were right, Goddess, your Mr Carey is a man to trust. None of this was his fault, after all. I blame myself in allowing someone to be my eyes who never saw anything but herself …"

"And had hysterics when the limelight was moved from her," Dieter said disgustedly. "I am glad to say Tom administered a hearty slap – that cut her off in mid-scream."

Liz felt her blood congeal. "*Melanie* threw a tantrum?" she asked when she could.

Dieter looked at her. "Of course … you would not know because you were not there. Yes, she was not the centre of attention, you see – everybody was quite naturally concentrating on my poor Maestro."

"Also she was still jealous because you had disappeared with Tom," the Don added. "That was why I tried to deflect her in the first place." He shook his head and pursed his lips distastefully. "I should have realised that there is no deflecting such self-obsession."

For the rest of the visit Liz heard nothing, but she must have made some kind of sense because nobody asked her what was wrong as she sat in numb horror, staring at the broken branch bearing the crushed remains of all those juicy conclusions she had jumped to.

It had been Melanie to whom Tom had referred on the telephone; *Melanie*, not Liz Everett. Hearing only one side of the conversation she had not understood that whoever was on the line had asked the whereabouts of the star of the show once Tom had said he and Liz were the only ones left at the villa. Still not wholly out of her drug-induced state she had stupidly thought she was the idiot he was referring to as throwing a tantrum, when a moment's common-sense reflection would have told her different.

*Oh, fool, fool – you and that destructive lack of self-confidence!* Any normal woman would have stormed into that kitchen and demanded an explanation. Not you. Oh, no, not Little Red Riding Hood. She ran away with her hands over her ears! Dear God, Liz thought, what *have* I done? No wonder he asked what was wrong. *I* was.

Subconsciously, she now saw with blinding hindsight, she had been preparing herself for the inevitable failure she was certain would arrive sooner or later. Had it not happened – more than once – to the two very attractive girls she shared with? So why should she be any different? She had been so convinced of her inability to hold a man so powerfully attractive to women as Tom Carey that she had *expected* to fail. With wilful blindness she had refused to recognise her triumph, even as it stared her out of countenance. Tom had meant it all: every single honeyed word, every soul-stirring kiss, and she had torn it into confetti before throwing it at him.

When she got back to the villa, Liz made straight for the telephone. She knew his home number; he had given it to her when she stayed behind at the villa in case he was out of the office should she need him. Too late she perceived that for the invitation it was. His phone rang several times before being answered. By a woman. Liz recognised the voice. Melanie's. She replaced the receiver without saying a word.

# Twelve

The Don left hospital the following Wednesday. A private ambulance brought him back to the villa, on his own, as he had asked them to remain there to welcome him back, and with his trademark champagne. They were therefore all gathered on the front terrace as the ambulance drew up at the foot of the steps. He was helped to alight, but he came up the steps jauntily, and unaided. He was not wearing his dark glasses, and apart from a square of sticking plaster over one temple, looked the same as ever. Except for one thing. He was not holding his white stick. This was not unusual since he knew the steps from long usage, but Liz wondered about it since it was steps that had put him in hospital in the first place. Evidently Adelina, standing next to her, shared her anxiety because Liz heard a sharply indrawn breath that ended in a gasp. Turning to reassure her she saw that Adelina's face was bone white but her eyes – her eyes were blazing! Crossing herself, she whispered worshipfully, "He sees! *He sees!*"

Liz whirled to the Don again and sure enough, as he neared her she saw that the black-olive eyes were a-glitter with triumphant life, but more than that, *they were smiling at her!*

Adelina flew at him, arms wide, laughing and crying. The Don embraced her for a few moments then held her away from him, his eyes drinking in her face with a look that had Liz swallowing hard, before kissing her with great tenderness after which there was an exchange of machine-gun Italian. Finally, with one arm around Adelina he stretched out the other to Liz as he mounted the last of the steps. As their eyes met and held she read in them confirmation of every word of his encouragement.

"I was right," he told her softly. "Even more right than I knew ..." Then, with a teasing smile again reflected in his eyes, he added, "Did I not say we would see?"

Later, when they were able to talk coherently, "How, when ... why?" Liz wanted to know.

"I will tell my tale, never fear," the Don

laughed, "but first let me have a glass of wine."

When it was in his hand he raised his glass to Liz. "To my young goddess, who has turned out in fact to be what I believed. I knew your coming was meant, in some way, but I must admit I had not foreseen this fantastic outcome. I salute you, and the fates which led you to me."

Later, when the first excitement had subsided, he told them what had happened. "It was really quite simple. My fall led to bleeding inside the skull which caused pressure. In operating to relieve it they somehow relieved other pressure which had been paralysing the optic nerve. It had not atrophied, as was thought, only been unable to function. Once the pressure was lifted it began, slowly, slowly, to come back to life. When I regained consciousness after the operation I knew something had happened because my darkness was not so complete; more grey than black, and that greyness paled with each day. I could not distinguish objects but eventually I became able to see shapes; blurred and hazy, but shapes nonetheless. I said nothing to the doctors because I wanted to be quite, quite sure. Once the haze cleared and I could perceive distinct outlines rather than blurs, I felt confident enough to tell them. They then examined me, shone lights in my eyes, scanned my brain, sat me in front of various machines, made me look at flashing lights and distant points, but their final verdict confirmed mine. Like a rusty machine my ability to see was creaking back to life, running itself in, so to speak. When you came to see me yesterday I could see your red dress, Adelina, Dieter's blond thatch of hair – and your smile, Goddess. However ... the light still hurts a little so I will put on my dark glasses. I have been advised to wear them for a while longer until I can face the light head on."

The ensuing days were high on excitement. Once the news was released the press besieged the villa, there were TV interviews, the telephone never stopped ringing and the mail was delivered by the sackful. Liz volunteered to deal with the latter, hoping that one of the many letters would be from Tom, and it was, but it was not addressed to her. The Don insisted on reading it to her – "now that I can." It congratulated him on recovering his sight and his health, and made the point that what could have been disaster had fortunately turned into a triumph. He wished the Don well and thanked him once again for the use of the villa. There was no mention of Liz or her eventual return to the Agency.

John Brittan did ring her, effusive in his praise for all the free publicity. "They are clamouring for the commercial, and I can tell you, my dear Liz, that having seen the first rough cut, it is a world-beater. That house! In combination with Melanie and your tantalising storyline it will sell the *L'amoreuse* line by the case! Needless to say the client is ecstatic! I cannot begin to tell you how grateful I am to you for persuading your friend to let us intrude on him. One could almost say it was fate. I mean, if Tom had not seen your sketch and you had not taken him to see the original, Mr diMarco might never have got his sight back! Now, you are not to worry about returning. Stay as long as you are needed. The Agency can manage without you in such a good cause."

*Amazing*, thought Liz. One minute manning the barricades, the next giving everyone a medal. She took no satisfaction from the praise she received. She had not been able to find satisfaction in anything since she had allowed her fears to overcome her fancies and sent packing the only man she had ever wanted. Mindful of the general air of miracles worked, she was careful not to show so much as a hint of her true feelings, but there was no fooling the Don, especially now that he had the use of his eyes.

"Something is troubling you," he tackled her one morning as they dealt with the piles of mail. "You are not still feeling the lingering traces of guilt?"

"No. I have no reason to feel guilty any more."

"Then what is it?"

Liz trotted out the excuse she had fixed upon. "I suppose it is the fact that I must think about returning to work. I have been here three weeks now, and you know what they say about all good things. My poor Empress will think I have abandoned her."

"So now you must abandon me?"

"You are fully recovered. Your regained sight is no flash in the pan and I am no longer needed."

"I have been thinking about that. You know I told you that they are pressing me to return to the concert platform? Well, I have now been offered a world tour, and I would very much like to have you along with me as my personal assistant. I have seen how well you organise, how capably and efficiently you handle things. I need someone like you to organise me and the thousand and one details of such a tour: travel arrangements, hotels, publicity, interviews, press conferences, rehearsals. I need someone I can trust, and who do I trust more than you?"

"Adelina."

"True, but she will be the third in our little triumvirate, to take care of my creature comforts which, as you well know, are important to me. It would mean leaving your usual type of work, but it would also mean seeing parts of the world as yet unknown to you. Think about it. I will apply no pressure, much as I would like to have your company as well as your skills, because I do not wish you to say yes out of a sense of obligation." He paused. "Unless, of course, there is something to keep you here?"

"No." Liz met the shrewd eyes head on. "Nothing at all."

"Then think about it. Be sure of what you really want to do."

So Liz got out her mental scales and proceeded to weigh the pros and cons. The pros were, as the Don said, travel – first class all the way – and a chance to see the world; the company of him and Adelina, now good and true friends both; the chance to acquire new skills. The cons were leaving work she loved. And Tom Carey.

Since that abortive phone call she had wondered if perhaps she was not grasping at more unripe conclusions. There were any number of reasons why Melanie should be at Tom's flat. Meetings had been held there before, she knew of them. There could be good, sound business reasons for her presence that night. As for the others ... Surely a man like Tom would not return to a woman he had spoken of in terms of disgust? Either way, until she knew for absolutely sure that her cause was lost, she would not be able to make up her mind. Only when she knew what his attitude was to her could she chart her course. So she told the Don she had to go up to London to settle one or two things. On her return she would give him her decision.

"Of course, I quite understand," he assured her, in such a way as to make it clear he understood everything.

She went to London next day, and on entering BB&B went straight to her own office. From there she rang Tom's. He was in the middle of a presentation, Mrs

Stephens said, an important one, and not to be disturbed. If she cared to call back in, say, an hour ... and in the meantime why didn't Liz drop by and give her a first-hand account of the *L'amoreuse* miracle play. Liz decided to go and have some lunch instead. Not at the *trattoria*; she did not want to have to satisfy the curiosity – or the gossip – of people to whom she knew she would still be a major topic of conversation, friends or not. She would go up to the sandwich bar on the corner. But she found she had no appetite. So she sat and drank a cup of coffee before making her way back to the office. The lift she rang for was on the top floor but descending, and when the doors opened out stepped Melanie, band-box fresh in sunshine yellow and looking very pleased with herself.

"Liz! Back from your adventures, then. What an exciting life you do seem to be leading ... a veritable fairy tale." Her smile said she did not believe in them before she returned to her favourite topic. "I know you will be glad to know that my own story also has a happy ending." She thrust her left hand under Liz's nose. "How about that, then?" she asked gloatingly. It was a star sapphire solitaire, obliterating the knuckle of her third finger.

"Congratulations," Liz was proud of her cool, steady voice.

"We are off to New York at the end of the week. We'll be married there, living there too. He can't wait to get back to the States. I mean, London is all very well, but New York …"

"When did all this happen?" Liz asked, showing just the right amount of bemused curiosity.

"Just last night. He made up his mind – snap," she clicked her fingers, "and refused to take no for an answer."

"Not that you had any intention of saying no."

Melanie looked askance. "Do I look crazy?" She admired her sapphire a moment then said: "Can't stop. Tons to do and not much time to do it in." Flipping her fingers she said, "Bye." And went on her way, all but dancing out of the building.

Liz went up to her office, where she sat down at her desk, took out a sheet of office stationery and rapidly wrote out her resignation, asking to be released immediately, if possible. If not, then she would take advantage of the four weeks holiday she still had due and use them as notice. She made two copies: one for John Brittan, the other marked for the attention of Tom Carey. Then she rang John Brittan's secretary and asked if it would be possible to see him. Twenty minutes, she was told. Which gave her time to go into her big storage cupboard and have a good cry before mopping her tears and re-doing her face to hide their traces. She was calm and composed when finally she presented herself on the top floor.

"He's still got somebody with him," John Brittan's secretary apologised. "Over-ran their allotted time. Have a seat, he should be out soon."

But Liz wandered over to the window where she stood staring over the river. When she heard the door to the inner sanctum open she turned, to see Tom Carey coming out of it. He looked at her. She looked at him. He did not smile. Neither did she. Then he nodded, as one does to an acquaintance, and made to move on but Liz found herself saying, "Congratulations."

He stopped, looked surprised. "You've heard?"

"Just now."

"It was supposed to be under wraps for a while longer."

"Nothing stays hidden in this place for long."

He frowned then as if remembering his manners, said, "And you? How are things? Things must have been pretty exciting at the villa these past couple of weeks. I read in the paper that *Il Signore* is considering returning to the concert stage."

"Yes. I am going with him. That is why I am here. To tender my resignation from BB&B."

His face did not change expression but she had an impression of tightening muscles. "I can't say that surprises me. Allow me to congratulate *you*." His voice was smooth, easy, empty. He moved then, towards the door but Liz said after him in a high, clear voice, "I don't suppose we shall see each other again, but I want to put the record straight by apologising for my bad manners the last time we met. I was ... upset."

"I know."

She managed to raise her arm, hold out her hand. "No hard feelings?"

He looked at her hand, then took it, held it for the moment their eyes met before saying quietly, "No." There was a pause. "None of them," he added.

Liz smiled at him, a brilliant, empty, rictus of a smile. "Goodbye, then," before turning blindly for the inner sanctum.

John Brittan was anything but happy to accept her resignation and tried every which way to make her rescind it. He offered her a sabbatical, a leave of absence, a raise in salary. She said no to all of them.

"Is it that you don't want to break in another Creative Director? I suppose you have heard that Tom is off to New York to set up a branch of BB&B over there ... It is supposed to be confidential but in this place even the walls have ears. He spoke very highly of you, very highly. You made a good team. I have seen the series of commercials, by the way, and they are every bit as good as promised: nominated for an award, in fact. You really do work so well together, you and Tom, the perfect partnership. Are you sure there is no way I can tempt you to stay? Perhaps you would like to go to New York too? I know he would be delighted to have you with him. I could arrange—"

"No," said Liz.

He knew that tone of voice. "Your mind is made up, then?"

"Yes."

He sighed. "Well, I suppose it is too good an offer to refuse, swanning around the world with a great singer. Just remember that if it palls, come back and see me. Promise me, now."

"I promise."

"Good." John insisted on offering her a glass of sherry, shook her hand warmly when she left and admonished her not to forget them. Liz went back to her office, emptied her desk, threw away what she did not want and packed what she did. She said goodbye to nobody. She knew she was not up to doing that. She would write to them, every member of her group, and tell them goodbye that way. She had enjoyed her almost eight years and learned a lot. Oh, yes. She had learned, all right. When she left the building it was without a backward glance.

She had not been gone ten minutes when Tom Carey came looking for her. She was gone. Room empty, waste-basket full. Something on the top of it caught his eye. One of her preliminary sketches of the villa. He picked it up, stood staring at it for a moment then, crushing it into a ball with a violent fist, flung it back in the basket before slamming out of the door. Almost at once it opened again and he came back in, retrieved the drawing, smoothed it out carefully and took it away with him.

# Thirteen

Nine months later, Elizabeth Everett sat at the Empire desk facing the big bank of windows in the sitting room of the elegant suite in the Carlyle Hotel in New York City, tapping into her laptop the final draft of the letter to be dispatched to those aspiring young singers judged worthy to attend the forthcoming summer's series of Master Classes to be given by the great baritone John diMarco.

New York was the culmination of their round-the-world tour, which had begun in London before crossing to Paris, to continue on through Europe via Germany, Austria, and Italy, before turning eastwards to the former Iron Curtain countries, whose reception had been rapturous, and Russia, where the diabolical fire in a voice undiminished by the years had set packed houses alight.

After St Petersburg and Moscow they had

continued east to China, of all places, where only one concert was permitted, but to an audience crammed into every vacant space of the great Hall of Peace, where the acoustics had caused the Don great aggravation, and then on to Tokyo, where everything was perfect. They then flew across the Pacific to Hawaii, where they enjoyed a relaxing ten-day break before continuing the tour in Australia and New Zealand. After six glorious weeks, the Don rested his voice by becoming a member of the audience at the Sydney Opera House, while Adelina and Liz rested themselves before tackling the most gruelling part of the trip: the coast-to-coast tour of the United States.

Over the past ten weeks the Don had sung his way across the country, beginning in San Francisco, at the Opera House, and proceeding east via every great city until tonight's grand finale at the Lincoln Centre, which would be the last in his series of three concerts, all of them standing room only.

So far it had been a triumph, not in the least for Liz herself, who had emerged as her own woman, having travelled a long way, physically and emotionally, from the hung-up, mixed-up girl who had burned her boats and thrown up a well-paid, secure job to hitch her wagon to a star who, charismatic or not, was a demanding man with a reputation as a womaniser, said to be conducting a *ménage á trois* which was *the* topic of conversation in musical circles, as well as the subject of much speculation. Liz had learned to cope with it, just as she had learned to cope with a great many things, not least the professional Don.

This one was an entirely different man from the retired one who, unable to see, had been resigned to sitting on the sidelines of life, amusing himself by stirring an idle finger in a nicely simmering pot or two. The professional man was a demanding perfectionist who expected the same from his entourage. As he saw it, it was his job to give an unforgettable performance to people who might only ever get to hear him once in their lives. That of Liz and Adelina was to see that he encountered no obstacle in achieving his aim. Thus these fantastic months had taught Liz to cope with just about anything, from delayed flights to misplaced hotel reservations, from ill-prepared dressing rooms to missing limousines, from a shortage of lemons for the Don's lemon and organic honey drink, always sipped exactly one hour before a performance to lubricate his voice to the loss of the special foam pillows on which he slept because he had once inhaled a feather from a duck-down pillow and it had played havoc with his throat. In the course of it she had had no choice but to acquire – at the double – every last bit of the confidence she had previously, and grievously, lacked.

Elizabeth Everett, cool, poised, *soignée* to the point where she intimidated, was not Liz Everett, with her blushes and blunders. It had taken her some time to get used to being at someone else's beck and call, but she was a fast learner, and by the end of the sixth week had devised her own system, one that had the diMarco machine running on the fastest of microchips and the ultimate in softwear.

The Don had sighed with satisfaction once he had appreciated her methods. "You see! Was I not right? You are as capable as you are captivating. With you to smooth my path professionally and Adelina to administer to my personal needs, was any man so well taken care of?"

That this was important to him showed in his singing. When things went well he sang like an angel; when they did not, hell had indeed no fury like the Don in a rage. Liz therefore did everything she could to ensure that there were as few glitches as possible, not always possible considering the logistics involved. She made a point of getting to know the Don's agent of many years, a shrewd operator who admired the way she kept the Don happy.

"I have to tell you," he complimented in his crisp New Yorkese, "you are one born organiser." She soon learned the importance of being in direct communication with the follow-on city even while the Don was singing in their current one, making sure that everything ordered, requested or specified, was ready and waiting. She developed an encyclopaedic knowledge of the differences between concert halls in the cities they visited, and became an expert on their telephone systems, even as she thanked God for e-mail and the fax machine.

She was quickly made aware of the snide comments whispered behind hands, the endless surmising done as to her presence on the tour and her place in the life of a man not shy of parading his conquests, but as she knew her position was way above board she did not let it worry her. Her dealings with the Don were scrupulously businesslike, though he made no attempt to hide his pride in and his paternal affection for her.

He allowed her a great deal of free time, encouraged her to go out with the many men who asked her, many of whom Liz soon realised had a hidden agenda; that of using her as a stepping stone to the greatest Don Giovanni of his generation, and he saw to it that she was always included on the guest list of the receptions, dinners and parties to which he and Adelina were invited. Tonight was no exception. After this final concert, his American impresario was giving a party in honour of a fantastically successful tour whilst already talking about arrangements for the next one.

Having finished the last of the Master Class letters, Liz then wrote her weekly letter to her father who, when she had told him her plans, had said only: "If you are sure it is what you want to do. But it is your life, after all, and you are old enough to know your own mind."

He – though not his sister who did not care for cats, or dogs come to that – had also been happy to take on Empress, on whom Suzie, his twelve-year old golden labrador, developed a definite crush, letting the Siamese boss her around mercilessly. Liz now wrote a swift two pages of news and gossip, the latter for her aunt, who liked nothing better than the inside track on anything appearing in the press or on TV.

That done, she printed and signed the Master Class letters, inserting them in their envelopes before putting them in the tray of mail which would be collected later. Then she stretched and checked her watch. She had thirty minutes before the business of the evening began. The Don was resting, as was customary before a performance. At six, Adelina would wake him with a raw egg beaten in brandy – he never ate before singing – then he would take a leisurely bath before dressing. At seven-forty-five the car would arrive to take them to the concert hall, where the final recital would begin at eighty-thirty sharp. His dislike of unpunctuality was well known. After the concert he would be the guest of honour at the party.

Picking up the remote control, Liz switched on the TV before putting her feet up on the sofa to relax for half an hour, keeping the sound low. The Don and Adelina occupied the adjoining suite but he was a light sleeper. The first channel she tuned into was showing a situation comedy, so was the second and the third and the fourth. She eventually found a news programme, but within minutes the commercials came thick and fast. These she watched with a jaundiced eye, even now comparing the different styles of advertising in America and the UK.

She sat up, though, as a familiar face appeared through the mist of a fountain she also recognised. Dave was right about its success, she reflected. She had seen the famous series of *L'amoreuse* commercials in just about every country they had visited, including Japan. She knew it had won awards and that Dave Barras was now directing his first feature film on the strength of it, but about the rest of them, including Melanie and her husband, Liz had heard nothing. After writing her farewells to all her friends in advertising she had deliberately cut herself off from that world. She wanted no reminders, but as the distance between her old and her new life grew, she found herself able to send the occasional postcard to the likes of Bertie Fry, John Brittan, Uncle Fred, et al. She had always been in regular contact with

Jilly, and it was to her she wrote her longest, wittiest letters.

On arriving in New York she had half-expected Melanie to look her up, to gloat if nothing else, but they had been here a week now, and nothing. It was not as though Melanie would not know, either, since there had been a lot of pre-arrival publicity, with yet more rehashes of the miraculous accident.

On reflection though, it was not surprising, Liz decided. She had apologised to Tom but the break had nevertheless been final, and she knew him well enough to know that no matter how much Melanie might like to gloat it was not his style. In which case what the hell was he doing marrying Melanie anyway?

*Now then*, she admonished herself, putting that particular genie back in its bottle, *you know by now how easily men are seduced by beauty. Yes, but ... well, I would have thought Tom, of all men, would want more than surface attraction. I could have sworn he was different. Well you were wrong. He isn't. Which is why he cut you right out of his life.*

Trouble was, whenever she looked under the bandage – which was as rare an occasion as she could manage – she found she was still bleeding. No other man had managed to staunch the flow, though quite a few had made the attempt; always she had found something wrong. She did not like one man's womanish mouth, another's peculiar sense of humour, a third's grating accent, yet another's hairy hands. Tom's mouth had been firm and clean cut, his hands well-kept and hairless, his voice deep and calming, his manner confident, his sense of humour akin to her own. No other man had ever penetrated her consciousness as deeply as he had, right from the beginning, or had his equally deeply disturbing physical effect on her.

If I were to meet him now, Liz thought on a pang, how different it would all be! I would have no difficulty in admitting now to all I could not find the courage to tell him then, such as my knee-jerk jumping to all those wrong conclusions. We could laugh about it, laugh about me. I could do it now. But you only get one chance and I made a hash of mine.

Switching off the television she went into her bathroom to run her bath, adding lots of fragrant bubbling oil perfumed with *Mitsouko*. Ever since that fateful night when Tom had said she smelled intoxicating she had never worn anything else.

She soaked for fifteen minutes then, wrapping herself in a towelling robe, set about doing her face and hair with all the confidence of her now fully realised woman-self. Spraying the air with a mist of *Mitsouko* she walked through it so that the fragrance clung to every inch of naked skin before putting on her Jewel Park bra and briefs under a dress that was a stunning fall of heavy white crepe suspended by shoe-string straps. Over it she wore a short, cardigan-type jacket of silver sequins which glittered under the light like the sun on water. She screwed single pearls in her ears and fastened a matching bracelet about her left wrist, before making a final examination in her mirror.

What she saw satisfied her, so picking up her envelope-type evening bag she checked its contents before walking across to the big double doors of the adjoining suite, on which she tapped softly before going through them. The sitting room was empty, but Adelina was in the bedroom, polishing the Don's patent leather shoes with a soft silk pad. She would not allow the staff of any hotel to so much as touch any item of his wardrobe. She knew what he wanted, how he liked it, and the right – the *only* – way to do it.

"Everything under control?" asked Liz in Italian, which Adelina had been teaching her.

"Yes. He is shaving."

"And the voice?"

Adelina smiled. *"Perfezione."*

"Good. I'm off then, to see that all is well at the Lincoln Centre. See you there."

Liz always went ahead; to check the dressing room, the placing of the piano, confer with that all-important man, the accompanist, for any queries he might have, inspect the tray laid ready for the Don when he came offstage; all and everything that might impinge on his mood when he finally arrived, precisely on time, dressed casually in slacks and a sweater, Adelina carrying his white tie and tails under a plastic cover. Once Liz had confirmed to him that all was as it should be, she retired to the box Adelina would later share with her, after she had helped the Don to dress, her final touch being the carnation in the buttonhole. As usual, she joined Liz just before the lights dimmed.

He was in magnificent voice and, his range being vast, he went from the chilling drama of Schubert's *Erle King*, to the haunting beauty of Duparc and the elegiac sadness of Hugo Wolf, lightening the mood with the elegant wit of Mozart and finishing with the bravura dramatics of Berlioz. The house rose to him and he gave them two encores, both American songs, after which the audience stood to clap and cheer long after he left the stage.

Adelina and Liz had left their box before then, so that by the time he entered his dressing room, his freshly poured glass of well-chilled champagne was ready and waiting to be put into his hand by Adelina. This he downed thirstily in one go. Only then did he take off his tailcoat and put on the more comfortable red-silk smoking jacket in which he would receive his admirers and fans, during which time, as he sipped at his second glass of champagne, Liz gave him a concise run-down as to the size and state of the house, along with the comments she had heard. Then, in spite of his exhaustion – he always gave everything he had to a performance – he received his visitors.

An hour later, when they arrived at the Fifth Avenue penthouse of his American impresario, it was to applause and acclaim, while Liz was herself the instant target of the usual coterie of grovellers and back-scratchers. These she dealt with easily, the result of much practice, and standing where she did, under the brilliance of a central chandelier, she seemed to give off her own light, since the thousands of tiny *paillettes* on her jacket reflected the light like splintering shards of glitter.

She looked magnificent, thought the man standing by the far windows overlooking the terrace. No trace here of the unsure, emotionally gauche and vulnerable girl who had hidden all this magnificence because she had no idea she possessed it. This woman knew her worth, and prized it. Taking the arm of the good-looking blonde by his side, he began a leisurely progress through the room, ostensibly with no goal in mind, merely having a word here, a laugh there, but in reality steadily making his way towards his objective until, as they reached it, there was an eddy in the group under the central chandelier as people moved away, allowing him to approach its centre and say, "I see you are living up to your title. Goddess indeed!"

The old Liz would have betrayed herself, this one said merely, "Hello, Tom," in a voice as cool and crisp as fresh snow.

They stood looking at each other, and the quality of the look and the silence had the group breaking up, drifting away, even the blonde who said, "I see an old friend of mine over there ... if you'll excuse me ..."

Neither saw her go. They stood facing each other like adversaries.

"You are even more beautifully frosted," Tom Carey said at last. "Obviously this life agrees with you."

Liz smiled and he felt it like a sword. "Yes, it does."

"No – regrets?"

She shrugged. "As Frank Sinatra sings in 'My Way', I've had a few ..."

"But you are still doing it your way?"

"Can you think of a better one?"

She was unfazed and he found he hated it. He had loved that innocent blush of hers; found it funny and endearing and touchingly sweet.

"I can see that life on Olympus suits you no end. What disguise did he use this time? I mean, he's used the bull and the swan and the shower of gold ... I know he said he was not Jove but we both know that for the 'little conceit' it was, don't we?"

That had her eyes igniting. "He uses no

278

disguises with me. I know him for all that he is."

"Well, that's a hell of a lot more than you would ever allow me to know about you. Every time I tried to get close, find out where your head was at, you gave me the brush-off. But I know your ... situation, now. Even so, I would not have thought you, of all women, to have taken it lying down."

For a moment her eyes were holocausts in a face that lost colour as if he had slashed a vein. He saw the hands holding her glass grip it tightly and tensed, expecting her to throw the contents at him. Instead, she turned on her heel and left him standing with egg on his face.

# Fourteen

From where she stood, the blonde, whose name was Shelley Anson, watched and saw it all: the strung-out tension, the wary body stances, the rigid facial expressions, the way words were flung like missiles. To her experienced eyes – she was an old hand in the Sex Wars having been married and divorced twice – it was all too familiar, as well as indicative of highly combustible emotions.

She had been aware of them in Tom the moment he set eyes on the statuesque beauty in the white dress. She had felt him tighten up, like an overwound spring, and had known instantly that this was the one for whom he carried the torch that she, Shelley Anson, had vainly been trying to douse for some time now, even though she had known there was Someone from the beginning. Tom had told her that on the night they became lovers, in that while he was happy to become her lover in the physical sense, there was no possibility of it including the emotions. So perversely – she never could resist a challenge – after being warned off she had fallen in love with him.

Now, she looked long and hard at the woman who had prior claim to Tom's emotions and wondered: what has she got that I haven't got, apart from an extra four inches and thirty-five pounds? What was it about *this* one that had Tom standing there looking like he was being stretched on the rack. Mind you, from the looks of her she was undergoing her own form of torture. No doubt about it, she decided on a sigh, this woman was why Tom was, so to speak, spoken for. In which case, she decided, while she did not give a damn for *her*, she was not going to stand by and let her carve up a man she, Shelley Anson, cared for more than somewhat.

Watching Liz Everett disappearing at a fast clip in the direction of the terrace – probably to cry her eyes out, she also saw Tom snatch a glass from a passing tray and empty it. And that is not the answer either, she told him silently. Which behoves me to find some answers of my own ...

Just then she saw the guest of honour, accompanied by the other third of what all

281

New York whispered was a definite *ménage-á-trois*, advancing on Tom, hands outstretched, as if towards a long-lost friend. Now was her chance. Quietly she made her way towards the big windows, open to the warmth of the spring night.

"Tom, my dear fellow … Adelina pointed you out to me as, of course, I never got to see you after I regained my sight. It is so good to be able to see what my goddess saw. But what are you doing in New York?"

"I work here now. BB&B opened an American branch and I run it. It was those *L'amoreuse* commercials we shot at your house which made it possible. What could have been a nightmare turned out to be a dream come true."

"Nicely put, but I never had any doubt that you would pull it off."

"Liz had a lot to do with it, but it does seem as though we have all got what we wanted."

"Indeed," the Don picked up the gauntlet at once. "I depend on my goddess for a great deal. I do not know what I would do without her."

"I do," said Tom.

They locked eyes, Tom challengingly, the

Don measuringly. Finally, as if making up his mind he smiled, nodded and said briskly, "I think it is time you and I had a little talk. It is long overdue and there are things you need to know. Adelina will excuse us." He took Tom by the elbow confidingly. "I have never told you how I came to meet my goddess, have I? It is a very enlightening story. Let me tell it to you ..."

When Shelley went onto the terrace, she could not see her quarry, but round the corner she knew there was a small sunken roof garden, hidden from the windows of the room where the party was being held by neatly clipped box bushes. Sure enough, there stood the tall blonde, hands clutching the low railing, staring out at Central Park.

As Shelley came up she did not turn, but after an instant's hesitation took the proffered clutch of tissues, mopped her eyes then blew her nose soundly.

"There is an automatic sprinkler system installed in this garden," Shelley advised kindly. "Your tears won't do much in the way of watering anything but that lovely dress." When Liz still did not reply Shelley sighed. "Dear, oh, dear ... I am encountering more wreckage tonight than ever surfaced after the sinking of the *Titanic*, not to mention that I have just seen my own hopes go down for the last time."

That got an armlock on Liz's attention. On a sniff she asked, "What do you mean?"

"I mean that beautifully designed, ocean-going yacht named the *Tom Carey*. You just torpedoed him."

Liz stared.

"Yes, the one and the same. *Your* Tom Carey."

Liz shook her head. "He's not mine. Never has been."

"Oh, yes he is. Whether you want him or not." Shelley paused. "But you do, don't you?"

Liz met a pair of dead level, knowledgeable, toffee-brown eyes, and knew the game was up. "Yes. I thought I was over him, that it was dead of starvation, but the moment I saw him …"

Shelley sighed. "How the old clichés come home to roost. But why does it always have to be in my loft? I came here tonight with him and I wondered why – since he goes to most junkets like this out of duty rather than devotion – he moved everything aside to come to this particular one, but the moment he set eyes on you I knew why. I

284

saw the way you went at each other in there. I don't know what was said but it was obviously lethal. People who have those sort of reactions are usually driven by powerful emotions and I'd say that between you, you are running a couple of thousand horse power. You have an effect on each other like the best quality sandpaper."

"Always rubbing the wrong way." Liz's voice came from the depths of despair. "He accused me of being—"

"Daddy's little sugar?"

Liz blew her nose again. "Which I am not. I work for the Don, end of story."

"Well, I have to tell you it's not the one that's circulating around town. In musical circles, the ones I go around in anyway – I'm a singer myself, but I sing in clubs, not concert halls – the theme of your particular trio is marked *'con amore'*."

"Then their score is wrongly marked. Adelina and the Don are a long-standing duet. Me, I only turn the pages. For some reason Tom always did have it in his head that the Don was grooming me to replace Adelina. As if he would! Apart from the fact that I do not want to replace her, the Don has no intention of doing so."

Shelley sat down on the flat top of the

wall. "Tell you what, why don't you tell me why Tom got it wrong?"

"Why should I do that?"

"Because if I am going to help you I need to know."

"Why should you want to help me?"

"Because in helping you I am helping Tom, and that is something I want to do very much. I am very – fond – of him. If he wasn't so hung up on you I'd have him pegged out on my line, but it's you he wants. Not for a moment has he ever felt for me what he so obviously feels for you, even though he has never so much as mentioned you in the time I've known him. I don't know what you did to each other – or didn't do, for that matter, but that torch he's carrying is by now bigger than the one carried by a certain lady out on Liberty Island."

Liz frowned. "But it doesn't make sense," she said. "Why would he marry Melanie if he was in love with me?"

"Come again?"

"Melanie – his wife?"

"Tom is not married. He lives alone – as I should know."

"But – they were having an affair and she showed me her engagement ring and said she was coming to New York and then I found out he was too."

"Did she say she was marrying Tom?"

"No, but ..." Liz closed her eyes and in a voice of flat despair groaned. "Oh, my God! I've gone and done it again." She put her head in her hands. "Why, oh why do I keep on doing it where he is concerned? Jumping to all the wrong conclusions?"

"Because love does that: unhinges one's mental processes, I mean. I know they say love is blind, but you two seem to have compounded it by wearing blinkers!"

"That was my trouble, unfortunately ... I lacked confidence in myself and thus, in Tom."

"So, tell me ... I like and respect him as well as love him, I want him to be happy, and if you are the means to that happiness, well, so be it."

"But – aren't you jealous? If it was me I'd be tearing your eyes out!"

"I've been there, and jealousy is destructive, not constructive. Besides, I've known for some time now that with Tom and me it is one-sided, tonight has finally shown me why. So, if I can't have his love I'll keep his friendship, and who was it said that was much more worth having than love anyway?

Come on," she patted Liz's hand, "tell old Shelley all, then we'll see what we can do about it."

Taking comfort from Shelley's non-judgmental understanding, Liz told her everything, down to the final meeting outside John Brittan's office.

"As I suspected," Shelley sighed, when Liz finished, "both of you so punch drunk you could not see straight. Talk about star-crossed lovers! Seems to me your eyes were crossed too! Time to kiss and make up, my girl, but not looking like that. Your eyes are a mess and your lipstick needs renewing. What you need is a restoration job, and I know just where to do it." Taking Liz back into the penthouse via another window, she led the way to a dressing room lined with mirrors above a bench with drawers beneath. Opening one of them Shelley revealed it to be a fully-kitted out make-up repository.

"You've been here before," Liz said.

"Many times."

Shelley sat and watched while Liz restored her face to its former perfection, finally being driven to ask, "You mean you really didn't wear make-up before? Absolutely nothing but soap and water?"

"Absolutely."

Shelley digested that then, watching Liz examine the finished product said roundly, "No wonder Tom was uptight after your transformation. He got beaten to the punch every time by that wily old fox, who probably flourished you at him like a trophy. You owe him a much delayed explanation, my girl. Is it any wonder he got the wrong impression when you repeatedly refused to give him the right one? Get yourself back in there and put him straight or you will have me to answer to. I know Tom, he is not a cruel man, and right now he is probably kicking himself for what he said to you, but you know what happens to a horse when a burr gets under its saddle. It lashes out in all directions. That is what Tom was doing. Now then, let's see how the repair job stands up."

Liz stood up, shook out her dress.

"Yes, you'll do, not that it matters. You could be wearing sackcloth and ashes and he would still think you looked like a million dollars."

When they went back into the enormous split-level living room they saw Tom and the Don, only feet away, talking intently, heads together. Adelina, who had been keeping an eye out, said something and both men turned to face the two women. Liz looked at Tom. He looked at her. And it was different. *He* was different. Hostilities had ceased and it was obvious he was more than eager to sign an armistice. Through her dizzying sense of relief and joyous anticipation she saw the Don slap Tom on the back, say something to him with a broad smile, while Adelina nodded encouragingly. Tom came towards her.

"He's all yours," Shelley said under her breath, "so handle him with care or you will have me to answer to."

As he reached them, Tom said to Shelley, still without taking his eyes from Liz, "I owe you one."

"I'll take a rain check," Shelley teased, before smiling in the direction of an attractively ugly man who had seen her and was moving in hopefully.

Tom took both of Liz's hands and held them tightly in his own. "We have a lot to say to each other, I think. Not here, though. Will you come with me?"

"Anywhere," Liz answered gladly. "Let's say our farewells ..."

"He knows," Tom said, glancing to where the Don, talking to an admiring group, was beaming at them. "So do I – now. I had it all wrong, but that's the way with jealous uncertainty. It distorts everything. I thought I'd lost every last hope a little while ago."

"Why do you think I was out on the terrace crying my eyes out?"

"Were you? I thought maybe you were plotting revenge! Can I plead temporary insanity?"

"You can plead anything you like, as long as it is in my courtroom."

As they rode the elevator they stood close to each other, smiling besottedly into each other's eyes, not speaking, Tom's thumb caressing Liz's palm, oddly and disturbingly arousing.

It had begun to rain, a light, warm drizzle, and they waited under the canopy of the building while Tom's car was brought round. As she got into it, Liz neither knew nor cared where they were going. All that mattered was that she was going with Tom.

When finally he stopped the car they were under a bridge and by a river: which ones Liz neither knew nor cared. As he turned to her she went into his arms like a homing pigeon.

After some time, Tom said in a blurred voice, "It's time we got off that roundabout we've been riding. I'm not about to lose on that what I've already lost in the swings. What went wrong that time at the hospital? What did I do or say that made you cut me loose?"

"Nothing," Liz answered. "I was the one who did and said all the wrong things, and all because I lacked the courage to come clean and confess."

"So ... confess ..."

Able to now, she admitted to all the wrong conclusions she had jumped to, making him wince and shake his head, but the last one really rocked him. "You thought I was marrying Melanie! Do I look crazy? Who or what in God's name gave you that idea?"

"Well, you were an item, and why else would she have been jealous of me?"

"My lovely innocent, she was ragingly jealous of you from the minute we saw you in that restaurant, but more important she also has a very finely tuned sexual radar which operates twenty-four hours a day, three hundred and sixty-five days a year. She knew the moment I began to have feelings for you – feelings that took me over as time went on. But let me dispose of Melanie once and for all then we can forget

292

about her. My remit where she was concerned was to keep her in line. She was the one who made the running as to how she expected me to go about it. My hormones are as normal as the next man's and she is a very beautiful woman. And that is all she wrote, because that is all there is to write about Melanie. She is a dead bore whose only interest is in herself. Besides, her long-term target was a much bigger fish than me. When she finally managed to hook him it was his rock she was wearing the day you met her. She'd just come from flourishing it at me. She is now Mrs JR-type-tycoon the fourth, living in Dallas, spending her time and his money in Neiman-Marcus."

"When I saw you tonight I did wonder why you were with another woman."

"Because Shelley was the one with the invite. She's a singer – and a damned good one; sings in the very hotel you are staying at. Oh yes, I know that. I know everything about you. I made it my business to; it was some kind of link even if the chain was broken. When I knew about the party I knew I had to see you for one more time."

"Thank God you did. We have wasted too much of that already on account of my

stupidity, but I'll make it up to you, I promise ..."

"I'll hold you to that ..."

"I'm counting on it."

"The Don also put me out of my misery tonight," Tom said contentedly sometime later. "So now I have the full picture. He is every bit as Machiavellian as I thought he was – and then some – but I admit I got it wrong where his reasons were concerned."

"We both got it wrong – me more than you because I had less experience with men than the average fifteen-year-old. I wanted so much to tell you how I felt about you but I just did not know how."

"Which is what I found so intriguing: the two people I sensed in you. From the start I had this feeling there was so much more to you than you showed, and once you came out from under all that burlap I could have killed whoever was responsible because I had so much wanted it to be me." He kissed her again as if to prove it.

Liz returned his kiss before saying, "While I lacked the confidence to tell you because I refused to believe you could be interested in me, of all people, and I knew that rejection by you would finish me for good."

"Tell me about it! I was positive you

shared my feelings because when I kissed you the night of the party your response was such as to write it in letters of fire. But at the hospital, you were so cold, so venomous. And even allowing for that damned electrician, Adelina's outburst and the shock you received I just could not understand why all of a sudden I was the guilty party and the sentence was exile to Siberia!"

Liz hid her face against him. "Don't remind me! Wrong conclusions yet again."

"No more of them, okay?"

Liz drew a cross with her forefinger. "Promise."

"Don't change anything else though, will you? I shall always love the unsure, little girl inside the confident big one." Framing her face with his hands, he said, "You are everything I want and need. I want to spend the rest of my life with you; go to sleep with you in my arms, wake up to see your face on the pillow. I want to look at you across the breakfast table, come home to you, fight with you, make up with you. Most of all I want to make love to you ... God how I want that ... but I also want you to know that you are the light of my life – and that has been losing power since you left it almost a year ago. You warm and you illuminate ... don't ever turn that light away from me, will you?"

In a shaken voice, Liz replied, "For you, I will even turn the other cheek."

They fell to kissing each other again unrestrainedly, their passion mounting. "I worship you," Tom murmured into her throat. "Isn't that what one is supposed to do with goddesses?"

"So do it, then ..."

"Not here. Let's go and love each other where we can do it properly, over and over and over again ..." He tipped her chin to look into her eyes. "My apartment is only a few blocks away."

Liz's smile promised him everything. "I thought you'd never ask!"